Credits

<table>
<tr><td>Author
John M. Stater</td><td>Interior Art
Andrew DeFelice</td></tr>
<tr><td>Developer
Bill Webb</td><td>Cartography
Robert Altbauer</td></tr>
<tr><td>Producers
Bill Webb and Charles A. Wright</td><td>Playtesters
Frog God Games Staff</td></tr>
<tr><td>Editor
Aaron Zirkelbach</td><td>Special Thanks
Bill Webb would like to thank Bob Bledsaw and Bill Owen for inventing the original hex crawl — the standard in wilderness adventure and a lifetime of fun.</td></tr>
<tr><td>Layout and Graphic Design
Charles A. Wright</td><td></td></tr>
<tr><td>Front Cover Art
MKUltra Studios</td><td></td></tr>
</table>

FROG GOD GAMES IS

CEO Bill Webb	**V. P. of Marketing & Sales** Rachel Ventura
Creative Director: Swords & Wizardry Matthew J. Finch	**Art Director** Charles A. Wright
Creative Director: Pathfinder Greg A. Vaughan	**The Maestro** Skeeter Green

Table of Contents

Hex Crawl Chronicles

— The Troll Hills —

By John M. Stater

There was a time when crystal domes dotted the landscape of the Troll Hills and sky sleds cut through the air like ships through the waves. That was long ago. The ancient, golden-skinned men, they say, built their domes too near the great lake from which all life sprang, and so the lake spawned the trolls and more fearsome creatures to punish the ancient men. Whatever the truth is, the ancient men were laid low, the cities crumbled, the survivors turned out into the wilderness and the hills were left to the trolls.

The Troll Hills are mostly gentle, rolling hills covered with green grass and dotted by woodlands of oak and hickory. They are bordered to the south by the Devil Peaks, jagged mountains that are home to the devilkins. To the north there is the Zarko Mountains, with valleys of pines where dwell dwarves in colorful coats who make rare distillations. The hills drain into the Sapphire River and Great River, which connects the Valley of the Hawks to Crescentium, the city-state of the witchmen to the south.

The Great River has proven a great boon to trade, but now the petty trolls have occupied the ancient fortress on Little Rock [3311] and shut down that trade, cutting Crescentium off from its markets in the north. Perhaps the adventurers might sally forth from north or south to open the river. Or maybe they'll ignore the wars of the trolls and witchmen and instead delve into the wilderness in search of the secrets behind the weird blue ruins of the ancient men.

The Troll Hills is a hex-crawl, referring to the hex-shaped units that divide the map. Just as dungeon adventures take place on a gridded map, wilderness adventures can be conducted on a hex map, allowing players the freedom to decide where their characters roam and giving them the thrill of discovering the many places and people that have been placed on the map. This map represents a large area filled with numerous places to discover and explore, and can be used as a campaign area in its own right, or dropped into an existing campaign. Referees can place adventures they have purchased or devised on their own into empty hexes on the map.

Adventures in the Wilderness

The hexes on this map are 6 miles wide from one side to the other. In open country, adventurers should be able to see from one side of the hex to another. In wooded hexes, vision is much more restricted. Random encounters with monsters should be diced for each day and each night, with encounters occurring on the roll of 1-2 on 1d6. The exact monster (or monsters) encountered depends on the terrain through which the adventurers are traveling. Unlike dungeons, in which the monsters on the upper levels are usually less powerful than the monsters on deeper levels, wilderness encounters are quite variable in their challenge, and low level characters face death every time they step out of the confines of civilization. Well-traveled adventurers will discover, however, that settled lands are not as dangerous as the rugged wilderness.

Hags and Trolls

Among the more pernicious and dangerous creatures in the Troll Hills are the trolls and their hag mothers. Most trolls are born from hag mothers and human or demi-human fathers. Under a full moon, hags are capable of appearing to males as nymphs in order to seduce them. Like some spiders, the hags usually eat male after they have mated. About one out of twenty troll births is a female that can breed true with other trolls. Trolls born from hags usually nurse from their mother for about two weeks, at which time they are about four feet tall and capable of catching their own food. The hag then drives the troll from its lair. Trolls return to their mothers from time to time to pay tribute.

Wilderness Random Monster Encounters

Roll	Hills & Valleys	Mountain	Woods	What Are They Doing?
1	Blink dogs (1d6)	Black bear (1d10)	Assassin vine (1d4)	Arguing Loudly
2	Dinosaur — Ornithomimus (2d4)	Devilkin ***	Dryad (1d8)	Fighting (roll another random encounter)
3	Dwarf (4d6)	Dwarf (7d6)	Ettercap (1d8)	Fleeing in terror
4	Giant badger (1d10)	Green dragon (7 HD) (1)	Giant skunk (1d8)	Hunting
5	Giant stag (1d6)	Giant goat (2d6)	Grizzly bear (1d8)	Lurking in ambush
6	Goblins (5d6)	Giant weasel (1d10)	Hag (1) *	Lying dead, bodies looted
7	Hag (1) *	Hag (1)* + Troll (1d4-1)	Human patrol (6d6) **	Making camp
8	Humans (4d6) **	Troll (1d6)	Owlbear (1d8)	Marching (random direction)
9	Sabre-tooth tiger (1)	Wolf (3d6) ****	Troll (1d4)	Reveling
10	Troll (1d4)	Wyvern (1d4)	Wild boar (1d10)	Searching for something

* Roll 1d4 to determine the hag's identity: 1 = Mother Rawbones [2703]; 2 = Black Bess [1510]; 3 = Old Grietje [2002]; 4 = Jenny o' the Green [1312]
** Human patrols are either witchmen led by a 3rd level fighter/magic-user or Xanlo river men led by a 4th level fighter or 3rd level ranger
*** Roll 1d4: 1 = Cackling devilkin; 2 = Moaning devilkin; 3 = Roaring devilkin; 4 = Screaming devilkin
**** 5% chance of a werewolf in the pack, in which case there are only 2d6 other wolves

Rumors

When adventurers are seeking information or rumors in a settlement or from the lord of a castle, you can roll a random rumor from the table below. Each rumor is either True ("T") or False ("F") and the hex number associated with the rumor is given in brackets.

Roll	True Rumors	Roll	False Rumors
1	The trolls have towers in the Devil Peaks	11	The goblins of the Troll Hills are poisonous
2	Beware the color blue!	12	Troblins are afraid of red-heads
3	There is a wondrous market in the Devil Peaks [Hex 0522]	13	When faced with a choice, always go left
4	The dwarves of Gundur will pay any price for tobacco [Hex 0901]	14	The primordial lake is an old wives tale – it doesn't exist
5	The Hundred Handed One sleeps in the Devil Peaks [Hex 1220]	15	The Valley of the Bear is a sanctuary for all [Hex 1503]
6	Black Bess likes pretty elf boys [Hex 1510]	16	The Crystal Temple holds the secret of eternal life [Hex 1805]
7	Some of the ancient folk escaped death and slumber beneath the ground	17	The trolls are working with the witchmen to conquer Xanlo
8	The Blue Fort is haunted by more than trolls [Hex 3014]	18	Mother Rawbones eats no meat [Hex 2703]
9	Fanglyn makes a fine gin, but don't make her angry [Hex 3223]	19	The Xanlo men are smuggling goods with the trolls – don't trust them
10	There is a secret entrance to Little Rock in the water [Hex 3311]	20	Elf women can bewitch a man with their gaze

Hags have an equally bizarre life cycle. A hag is an elven women that has reached their allotted 1,000 years of life as an elf. At this point, lawful elves wander into the woods and become nymphs. Neutral elves find a nice oak tree and turn into dryads. Chaotic elves crawl into a damp burrow or fallen log and cover themselves with mud and leaves. After one month, the elf emerges as a hag.

The three hags who gave issue to the petty trolls have recently come together to form a covey and spread their dominion over the Troll Hills and maybe beyond. These hags, Peggy Blackteeth, Mollie Longshanks and Fat Anya, because they have formed a covey, can now cast the following spells three times per day each: *Animate dead*, *control weather* and *phantasmal force*.

Humans

The **Golden Men**, first introduced in *HCC 1 – Valley of the Hawks*, can be found in the western portions of this hex crawl. Descendants of the ancient men who once ruled over the Troll Hills, the golden men dwell as hunter/gatherers in the woodlands or on the prairie, hunting smilodons, brototheres, mammoth and other big game. The golden men know next to nothing of their heritage, so they cannot be depended on for technical assistance with the relics of their forebears. The golden men have golden-brown skin (hence the name) and flaming red hair. Warriors wear leather armor and carry stout clubs and leather slings or metal weapons scavenged from their victims.

The **Witchmen** have tan or olive skin and a great variety of hair and eye colors. They wear long, straight tunics and woolen leggings. Their shoes are leather and pointed, and they wear tall pointed hats with wide brims; both shoes and hats are decorated with buckles of brass or silver. The witchmen carry long swords and daggers, and wear either ring armor or chainmail. Their leaders are skilled in swordsmanship and magic, and should be treated as elves in terms of special abilities and class choices.

From the great river port of Xanlo come the **Xanlo River Men**. The river men are the result of mixture between the southern Witch Men and the Northern Men introduced in HCC 1 – Valley of the Hawks and detailed in HCC 4 – The Shattered Empire. Xanlo river men are of medium build and height, with creamy brown skin, wavy black hair and sparkling eyes of dark orange or amber. They usually wear ring armor and carry staves (attack twice per round), crossbows and daggers.

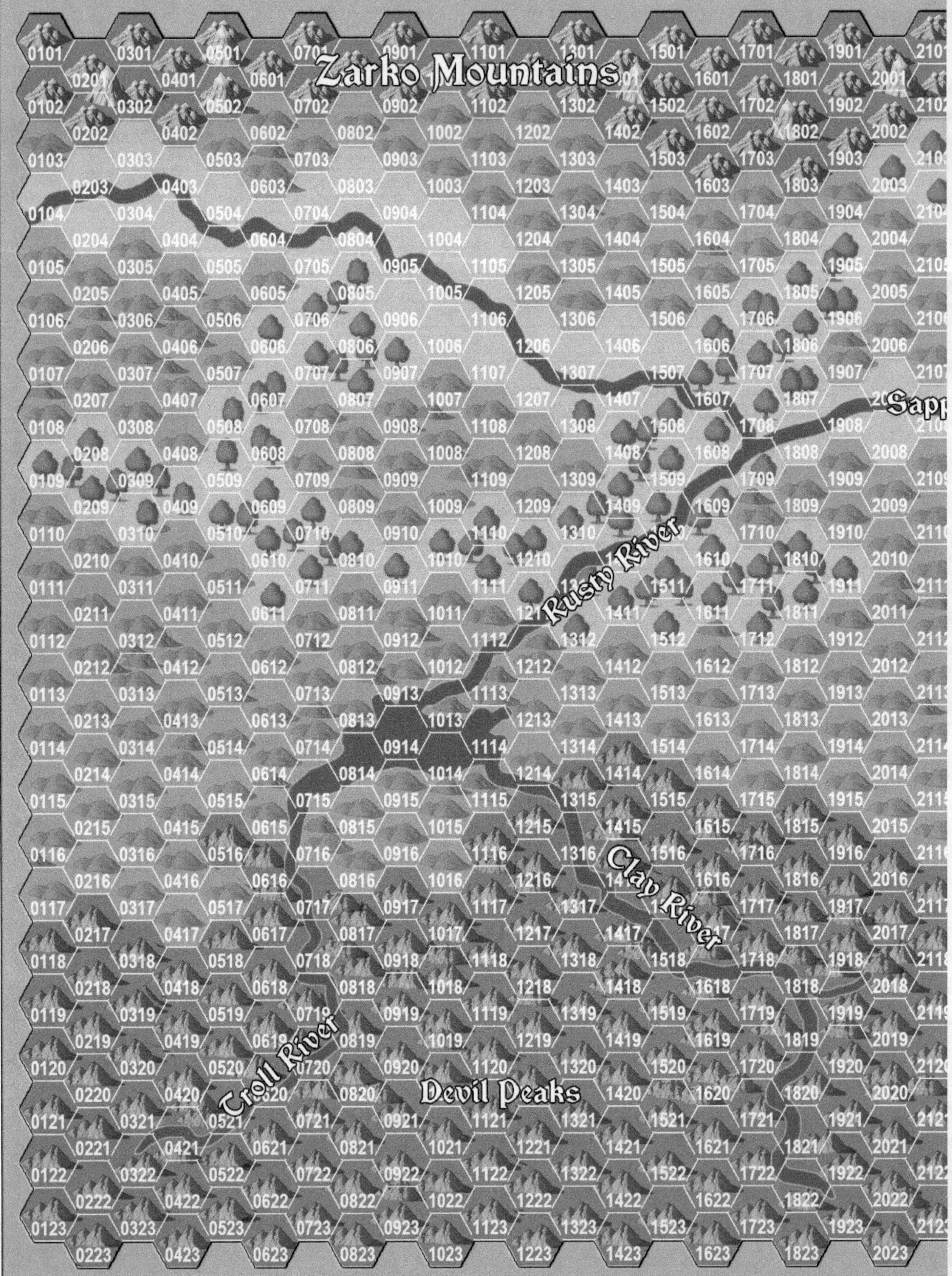

Zarko Mountains
Rusty River
Clay River
Croll River
Devil Peaks
Sapp

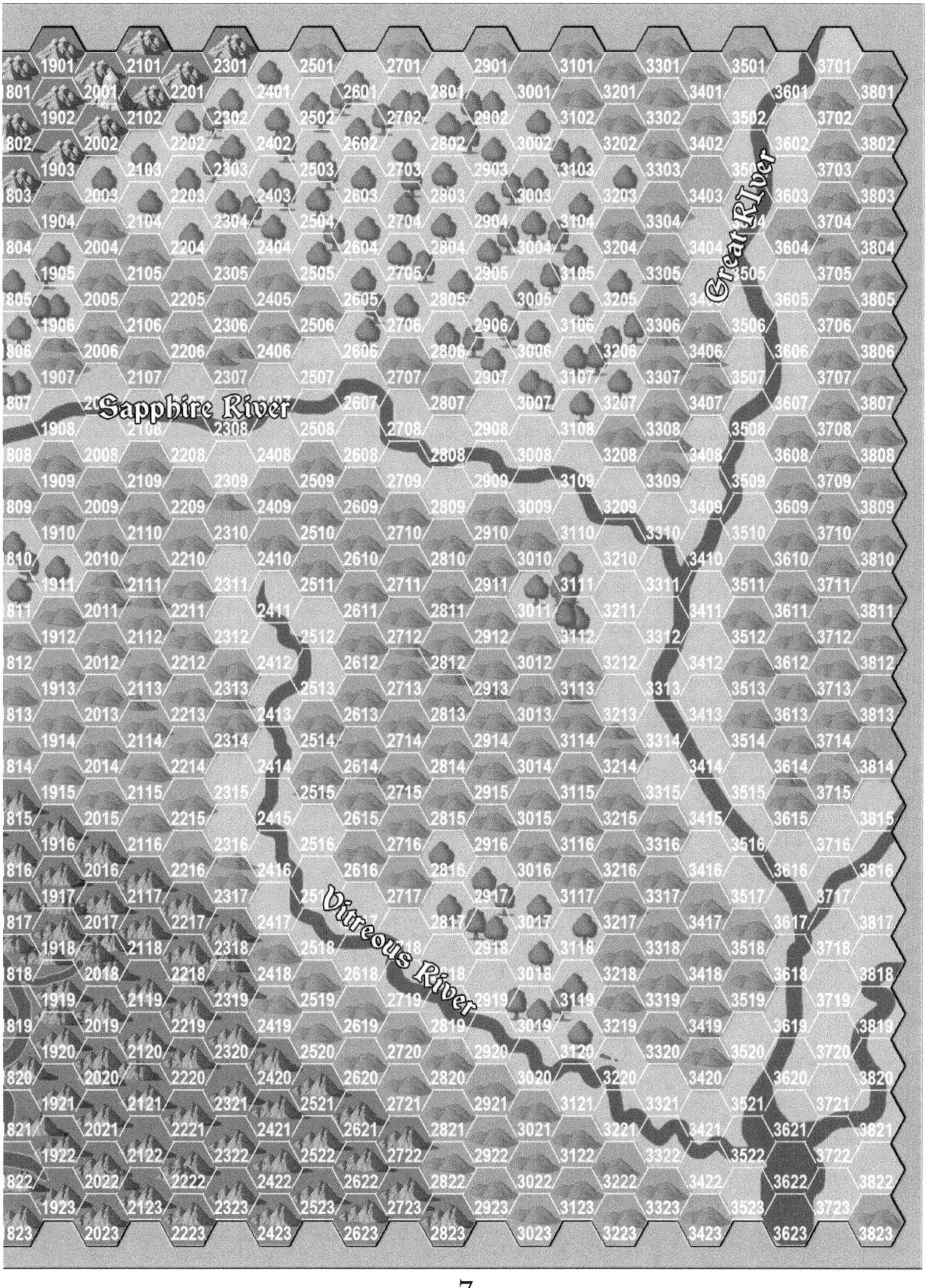

Great River
Sapphire River
Vitreous River

Demi-Humans and Humanoids

The trolls don't make for very good neighbors, so few other intelligent folk dwell in the Troll Hills. The goblins of the region are mud-dwellers, living in the mucky river valleys and burrowing into the mud. They have white, fish-like flesh and only come out of their mud burrows at night. The goblins fear cats and owls, despise witches and carry bronze spears and daggers.

The Zarko are home to a breed of dwarves usually referred to Zarko dwarves. The Zarko dwarves dress in long, colorful, stitched coats and generally present a more jovial appearance and attitude than their fellows elsewhere. They are known for chewing on licorice root, keeping bees (they make a tremendous mead), mining lead and iron and distilling moonshine. To make moonshine a dwarf must gaze on the full moon and allow a tear (of joy or sadness) to come to his eye. These tears are collected and distilled and the result is put into oak barrels. When sipped, it acts as a restorer and healing potion but also inflicts 1d6 points of wisdom damage for 24 hours. Zarkos are born fiddlers and dancers.

Few elves still dwell in the Troll Hills. Most are visitors from the north. The northern elves are trouping fairies who dress in rich clothes of mauve, cyan and soft green and who wear gleaming armor and carry lances and swords.

The Blue Plague

The blue plague is a strange disease lurking in the ruins of the Ancient Men. The disease covers the face and arms of the afflicted in blue-black splotches and causes their tongues to swell and distend out of their mouths. It inflicts 1d4 points of constitution damage each day, making a person fatigued and irritable. Symptoms appear when the person's constitution score has been reduced by half. At this point, the afflicted person loses the ability to digest normal food and must seek out the weird, blue flesh and vegetation found around the Blue City or continue to lose constitution. People who starve to death rise as blue-skinned ghouls 24 hours later.

Encounter Key

0113 Throat Leeches:

In the rolling, undulating hills, among the tall, green grasses there are a number of tall, granite outcroppings. One of them, in this hex, has been carved to resemble a large drinking horn. Lapis lazuli has been inlaid into the rim, and the stone now holds a quantity of water. The frequent rains keep the water somewhat fresh (assume a 35% chance of fresh water, otherwise stagnant), but it is unfortunately inhabited by throat leeches. A passing thief, on the run from a war party of ancient men, dropped a lockbox into the horn. The box contained a treasure map on oil cloth as well as a large emerald worth 1,600 gp. The treasure map shows the location of the old bunker in the ruined city [1507].

0119 Mollie's Tower:

A cleft in the mountains here is filled with junipers which obscure the existence of a tower keep made of granite blocks with a crenellated roof and five hexagonal towers (53-ft tall), each one topped by a conical roof of beaten bronze. The walls of the keep are 43 feet tall. The battlements are ever watched by patrols of 1d4+3 petty trolls garbed in leather armor and carrying spears and throwing axes. Because the petty trolls have been collected at the Little Rock [3311] with their mother, only about fifteen of the sons of Mollie Longshanks [2421] remain in her fortress. There is no treasure here save a few odds and ends and a locked iron box buried beneath the floor stones in Mollie's brooding chamber. This box contains

a *flute* of black metal entwined with gold thread. The flute can be used as a *+1 light mace*. It glows when played and can be used to turn oozes as a 4th level cleric turns undead.

0122 Bunker:

A cement bunker built by the ancestors of the ancient men was built into the mountains here. The bunker is constructed of cement. There is a lower portion that contains two separate iron doors, both extremely difficult to open (open doors as though strength 5 points lower or -20% to thief's open locks check). The upper portion consists of a control room with thick glass windows overlooking the mountain valley. The control room is dusty and dilapidated. Its energy source, an atomic pile located deep underground, long ago failed, irradiating the caverns beneath the mountains and filling them with unspeakable horrors. The application of raw electricity has a percentage chance equal to the level of the magic-user using it to spark the controls into life for 1d6 turns. During this time, one can fool with the controls (see diagram below). Each round roll 1d8 plus the person's intelligence bonus to discover which even is triggered:

Roll	Event
Up to 1	Poison gas released into room. All present must save or suffer 2d6 points of damage.
2-4	Alarm klaxons sound, attracting a wandering monster in the hex to the bunker to investigate.
5	Air conditioning turns on.
6	Voice warns of core meltdown in 10 seconds. Adventurers probably will not understand the voice, which is okay since there is no longer a core to melt down.
7	Blast shields cover windows and all doors lock. If air conditioning is not on, oxygen runs out in 1 hour.
8 or higher	Missile launch! Unfortunately, those systems no longer work other than to arm the missiles, which are in silos beneath about 10 feet of rubble on the valley floor below the windows of the bunker.

The control room is guarded by three wights garbed in silvery radiation suits (that do not block their powers). These suits are torn and tattered, and so provide no protection from radiation or other energies. Two suits in a closet here, however, do provide a +2 bonus to saving throws against fire, electricity and cold attacks. There are also three power rods of the ancient men in the room (treat as magic wands with 1d6 charges) capable of unleashing a copper-colored ray that inflicts 1d6 points of damage or a scarlet ray that forces one to pass a saving throw or fall asleep (per the spell).

WIGHT: HD 3; AC 5 [14]; Atk 1 claw (1hp + level drain); Move 9; Save 14; CL/XP 5/240; Special: Drain 1 level with hit, hit only by magic or silver weapons.

0201 Rune Slab:

A flat slab of stone nestled behind black walnuts is covered with runic inscriptions and weird diagrams that look something like angular demons emerging from sunbursts. The runic inscriptions are a sort of riddle, "Hold and behold, gentle seeker of knowledge, should you wish to enter this portal." One can only open this portal by casting *hold portal*. This causes a seam of blue light to appear in the slab, which can then be wedged open using crowbars or similar objects and open door checks. Behind the slab there is an 80-foot long tunnel of blue stone that descends at a sharp angle.

[A] This chamber has glassy walls with a blue sheen. In the center of the room there is a statue of a woman with a mouse's head and slim arms with hands outstretched. Hanging from the hands of the statue there is an amulet on a gold chain. The amulet has the shape of a walled city. When adventurers first walk into the room, choose four of them. Everything

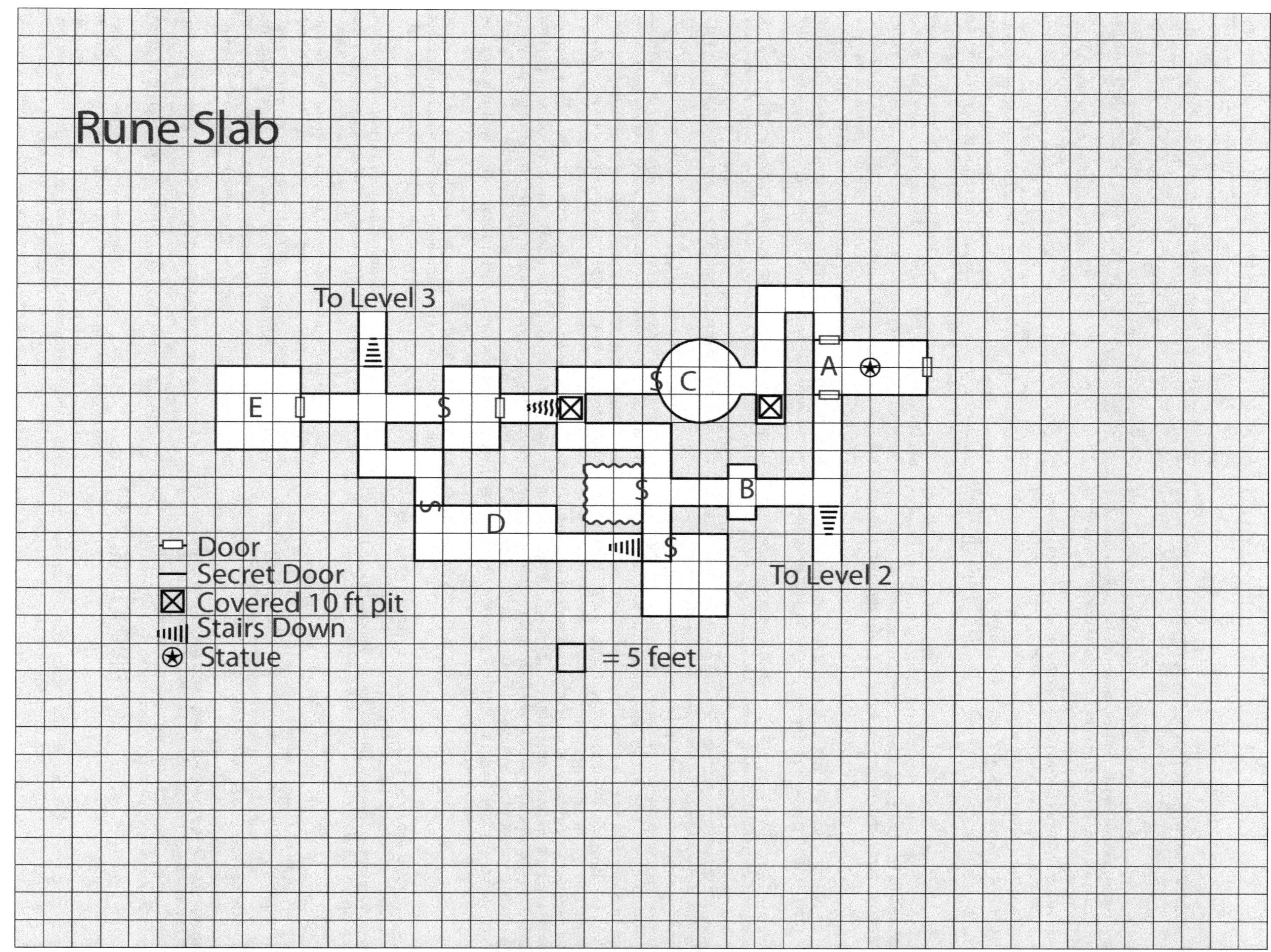
Rune Slab
To Level 3
To Level 2
E
D
C
B
A
Door
Secret Door
Covered 10 ft pit
Stairs Down
Statue
= 5 feet

these adventurers look at is projected on one of the glassy walls in great magnification. By closely examining the amulet, they can discern what appear to be miniature people tormented by swarms of rats. If removed from the statue's hands, a swarm of ethereal rats emerge from the glassy walls and attack the holder of the amulet. If replaced, they continue their attack on the perpetrator until he or she is dead. If worn around the neck, the amulet gives one the power of a wererat. If worn from one full moon to another, the amulet actually turns the person into a wererat.

ETHEREAL RATS: HD 2; AC 6 [13]; Atk 1 bite (1d3 + ethereal poisoning); Move 9 (C9); Save 16; CL/XP 4/120; Special: Ethereal poisoning, etherealness, surprise (4 in 6).

[B] This corridor has smooth walls. In the center of the corridor there is a chamber with a domed ceiling. The walls here are fluted. Hanging from the ceiling there is a large gong. The gong reaches nearly to the ground and is 6 feet in diameter. The first person to step into the chamber finds themselves pushed by an invisible force (saving throw to negate) into the gong, making a colossal noise. The victim suffers 1d6 points of damage. All people within 20 feet of the gong must pass a saving throw or be deafened. Once the gong is sounded, it is impossible to surprise any monsters on the first two levels of the dungeon.

[C] This circular chamber is clad in reddish stone. In the center of the room there is round, steel plate 3 feet in diameter. Floating three feet above the plate there are five steel orbs. The orbs float within 9 inches of one another in a pyramid shape. They cannot be moved more than 9 inches away from or 9 inches closer to their fellows. A second steel plate is affixed to the ceiling. When somebody touches an orb, an invisible tube of force is created between the two steel plates, trapping people inside with only one hour of air. If the orbs are put into a circle on a plane even with the ground and spun, a silver bastard sword slowly appears in their center. Grasping this *+1 bastard sword* causes the force field to vanish. The sword allows the wielder to change his appearance to that of any humanoid creature from whom it has drawn blood (i.e. done at least 8 points of damage). The sword, called *Bazalti*, draws its power from its wielder's love of glory and does its best to push them into acts of daring-do. Unfortunately, it also causes a mild paranoia in its owner – they can never fully trust another person.

[D] This long gallery features three small alcoves set 8 feet above the floor. Each alcove is 2 feet tall and wide and three feet deep with a leather satchel pushed all the way to the back. The room is guarded by Odweal, a shadowy panther-like creature with six legs. Odweal's fur is absolutely black, allowing it invisibility in darkness. Odweal can use the following spells as psionic powers: *Darkness 10' radius, ESP* and *hold person*. He can also emit a psychic pulse that forces all within 20 feet to pass a saving throw or suffer 1d6 points of damage and be stunned for 1 round.

The satchel in the left alcove holds a silver, human-sized arm. If held to a bleeding stump, it fixes itself to the body and operates as a normal arm (though it sometimes has a wicked mind of its own). This is convenient, since the left alcove also holds a guillotine that lops off any arm that reaches inside (2d6 points of damage).

The right alcove hides a golden mask depicting a gorgon. If affixed to a damaged face, it affixes itself and acts as a real face. It makes the person immune to poison gas and allows them to see in darkness, but also imposes a -4 reaction modifier due to its unnerving gaze. The mask is also convenient, since a nozzle in the back of the right alcove spews forth an acidic gas that inflicts 2d6 points of damage when pressure is placed on the threshold of the alcove.

The central alcove holds an iron ingot.

PSIONIC CAT: HD 8 (37 hp); AC 5 [14]; Atk 2 claws (1d4) and bite (2d4); Move 18; Save 8; CL/XP 10/1400; Special: Psychic powers, invisible in darkness, psychic pulse.

[E] This laboratory has a dozen stone tables holding glass tubes, alembics and braziers keeping the liquids therein bubbling. A large bell jar holds a weird, ooze-like creature that glows in tones of red, gold and blue. The creature within the glass is a captured phasm that wishes only to escape, though it may attempt to communicate with its rescuers and even

stay with them long enough to escape the dungeon.

PHASM: HD 15; AC 2 [17]; Atk 1 strike (1d4); Move 12; Save 3; CL/XP 16/3200; Special: Shapechange into any creature up to 12 feet tall or long, immune to poison, sleep, paralysis and polymorph.

0204 Blue Obelisk:

There is a 30-ft tall obelisk here made of blue stone. There are four small holes in the base of the obelisk, each one surrounded by a ring of colored metal – blue, green, red and white. The base of the obelisk is granite and is carved with ancient runes that proclaim it the home of Morgil, the thunder goddess of the ancients. By placing gems of the appropriate color and worth at least 1,000 gp in the four holes in the base, the blue obelisk shifts into the ethereal plane and is replaced by the image of Morgil.

Morgil is a 20-ft tall woman, graceful and elegant, with slanted azure eyes and porcelain skin. Her red hair hangs nearly to her ankles and she wears a robe of blue scales. In her hand she carries a silver flute with which she calls the winds and rains. The image will glare at the assembled, awaiting the proper rituals and chants. When they do not occur, the sky quickly fills with swirling clouds, pouring rain and the equivalent of a double-strength *call lightning* spell. If proper worship is given, the goddess image will answer four questions per the *commune* spell.

0308 Box Canyon:

The hills here are rougher than most of the gentle hills here. They are covered in scrub oaks and poison ivy and form many box canyons. One of these canyons holds a shrine of Alberni, the moon goddess. The wall of the canyon is carved in her image – a dog-headed woman with silver eyes and mouth agape. The mouth is a tunnel into a cramped shrine containing an idol of the goddess presenting her foot to be kissed. Those who fail to do so suffer a curse (save or -2 to all d20 rolls until 300 gp worth of incense is burned at her altar in the ancient, ruined city [1507].

Beneath the shrine, under a hidden trapdoor, there is a temple complex that includes living cells for the diabolical priests of Alberni, all ancient men garbed in wolf-skin loincloths and carrying clubs. Each cell is furnished with a black bowl of unholy water, ancient, faded magenta curtains and cushions stuffed with poppies. The remainder of the complex (storage rooms, meditation rooms, etc) is patrolled by horned apes with black hair and magenta skin. The inner sanctum of the temple contains a full idol of the goddess that breaths hallucinogenic fumes that cause insanity in about 1 in 100 people.

HORNED APE: HD 5; AC 6 [13]; Atk 2 claws (1d4) and 1 horn (1d8); Move 12; Save 12; CL/XP 5/240; Special: Hug and rend.

DIABOLICAL PRIEST: HD 3; AC 8 [11]; Atk 1 club (1d4); Move 12; Save 14; Special: Immune to fear, summon 1d4 wolves (takes 1d4 rounds for them to appear), cast spells as 5th level cleric.

0311 Troll Lair:

A wooded dell here holds a small, wooden fortress inhabited by six trolls and their mother, an annis hag called Stappa the Old. Stappa has haunted these hills for almost a millennium and remembers well the ancient men, their fabulous machines and the looks of stark terror on their faces when first they met her. Stappa's sons mostly hunt the hills looking for razorback hogs and the odd ancient man they can bind and carry back to entertain mother. Stappa dwells in a stony cave beneath the fortress with her collections of scalps and jars of human organs preserved in alcohol.

TROLL: HD 6+3; AC 4 [15]; Atk 2 claws (1d4), 1 bite (1d8); Move 12; Save 11; CL/XP 8/800; Special: Regenerate 3 hp/round.

0313 Troblins:

One hundred troblins dwell here on a butte covered by pines. The troblins hunt rats and consume cakes made of fermented honey, for the meadows on the butte are home to a wondrous variety of wild flowers. At the heart of the troblin village, constructed of long, wooden houses with thatched roofs, there is a weird idol of red, porous rock the troblins call Ky'loo. Ky'loo vibrates on a strange frequency that makes elves nauseous and dwarves amorous. Ky'loo is covered with stone spikes on which the troblins sacrifice folk that fall into their possession. The troblins of the butte wear skull caps and puce cloaks and carry flails and shields.

TROBLINS: HD 3; AC 8 [11]; Atk 2 claws (1d4) and bite (1d6) or weapon (1d6) and bite (1d6); Move 9; Save 14; CL/XP 4/120; Special: Regenerate 2 hp/round, mutation.

0317 Springal:

An old springal (a siege engine used to cast arrows) lies here in a small crater. The springal has a broken axle and wheel. It is surrounded by speckled toad stools that are highly poisonous and, more importantly, sprout on the broad back of a large creature that looks like a giant mole. The mole thing has been hibernating for several years and would like to hibernate for many more. He'll be grumpy if jostled awake.

MOLE THING: HD 9 (32 hp); AC 5 [14]; Atk 2 claws (1d8); Move 9 (B6); Save 7; CL/XP 9/1100; Special: Can sense things up to 30 feet – blind otherwise, immune to charms and illusions.

0502 Healing Shrine:

A conical shrine of mossy field stones is stacked next to a bubbling mineral spring. The waters have no healing power if ingested (in fact, they'll make a person terribly ill for 1d3 days). But, if a wounded body part is molded in the clay soil that surrounds the spring and tossed in, that body part will be healed (i.e. cure disease or up to 3d6+3 points of hit point damage healed). This healing is performed by the ghost of the shrine's former priestess, Amrantha. When the moon is full, Amrantha appears sitting on the banks of the spring, gazing at the moon. In this form, her touch causes one to age 1d6 years (2d6 for halflings, 5d6 for dwarves, 10d6 for elves).

AMRANTHA: HD 7; AC 3 [16]; Atk 1 touch (1d6 chill damage + level drain); Move F15; Save 5; CL/XP 10/1400; Special: +1 or silver weapons to hit, touch drains one level (save negates).

0515 Spiral Smoke:

A spiral of smoke erupts from the ground here, which is dry, scorched and cracked. The smoke originates in a clearing 30 feet in diameter surrounded by stunted trees hung with rope-like strands of brown mold. The chill from the mold is apparent when one comes within 10 feet of the clearing and vanishes by the time one passes through to the smoke (though then they must contend with the acrid smoke). The ground from which the smoke originates is about 3 feet in diameter and provides no hand holds. At the bottom of the hole there is a hemispherical chamber of blue glass and tunnels that head toward the ruined city in [1507] and the bunker in [0122]. There is no light here. The floor holds a thick, copper cable embedded in the glass. The smoke originates from a break in the copper, which spits electrical arcs that seem to feed on the very air (folks getting too close must pass a saving throw or become dizzy and maybe, if their constitution is 8 or less, fall unconscious for a few minutes). Encounters in the tunnels occur on a roll of 1 on 1d6 per hex and should be made on the Blue Ruins table above.

0518 Kamoo:

Kamoo is a fortress of the ancient men nestled among the pines. The fortress houses 200 people who support themselves by hunting in the woods and catching fish in the streams. The fortress is actually a partially ruined resort building of the ancient men. The building is five stories tall and a city block long. It is made of brown stones and highly ornamented, though a few centuries of weather has eroded much of this decoration. The ground floor holds a great hall (once a lobby) used as a throne room by the chief and his notables. There are also kitchen and dining facilities. The upper floors house the men and women of the tribe. The chieftain, Talman, is a hefty man who wears brass rings and bangles on his arms and in his nose and ears. Excitable and surly, none cross his path. All of the men and women of Kamoo are capable of charming the animals of the woodlands with a strange whistling noise.

TALMAN, FIGHTER LVL 6: HP 24; AC 6 [13]; Save 9; CL/XP 6/400, Special: Multiple attacks, parry. Leather armor, spear, short bow, dagger.

0522 Trading Post:

Archimages from all over Namera know of the wondrous trading post situated here by the river. The post is constructed of stone and consists of a rectangular building of coppery stone surrounded by colonnades and topped by a dome that glows with golden radiance at night. During the day, the building has no entrance – no windows, no doors, etc. At night, though, one can enter the dome, which becomes immaterial. Underneath the dome there is a wondrous plaza of black bricks thronged by magic-users and magical creatures from throughout the multiverse trading secrets, spell components, odds and ends of conjuring and the occasional insult (though no offensive magic is permitted, with guilty parties set upon by a gang of three clay golems in the shape of tall, robed men with primitive foreheads, aquiline noses and long beards of black ringlets.

It is up to the Referee what items are sold here – perhaps potions and scrolls, but any other magical items should be extremely rare and very expensive (i.e. in the range of 2d6 x 10,000 gp). Magical ingredients, ornaments, tools, etc should certainly be available, and private rooms where magic-users can swap spells also make sense.

0607 Sculpted Wall:

A concrete wall cuts through the woods here. The wall is about ten to twelve feet tall and fifty feet long. A bas-relief of two armies – perhaps gods in battle – is imprinted on the wall. Pits where burnt offerings left by the ancient men can be seen before the wall, and many oracle bones have been cast beneath the warriors. The woods around the wall are infested with giant ticks, and 2d6 are encountered by those poking around the wall.

GIANT TICK: HD 3; AC 4 [15]; Atk 1 bite (1d4); Move 3; Save 14; CL/XP 3/60; Special: Drain blood.

0611 Cunning Trap:

A group of gnomes have dug a pit here to capture the dire wolf that has been threatening their woodland home. The pit is shrouded in illusion, and appears to be a struggling deer on the woodland floor.

0620 Rope Bridge:

The swiftly rushing river here can only be crossed via a rope bridge. The bridge is sturdy and not remotely dangerous unless someone speaks while crossing the center of the bridge. Any utterance causes the bridge to suddenly snap its moorings on both ends and rotate so that it is even with the river. The ends now intersect with invisible pocket dimensions. The far end of the bridge now reaches into a scarlet portal that pulses and spits sparks. The near end ends in a purple radiance that vibrates and hums. 1d4 rounds after the bridge turns, files of soldiers come out on the bridge prepared to do battle. From the scarlet portal come twelve manes demons in service to the anti-cleric Endrad the Evil. From the purple portal come the twelve medusa brides of Karran of the Unspoken Oath, resplendent in armor of blue scales and wielding short bows and curved swords. The combatants care not if they destroy innocent bystanders, and the bridge cannot be turned until one side has been driven back into its own portal.

Stepping through the scarlet portal brings one into a complex of scarlet passages and chambers inhabited by the devil worshipping Endrad and his servants. The purple portal opens into a plain of purple sands and coral sunsets that holds an airy pavilion of white silk curtains and luxurious couches where lounges the blind wizard Karran.

MANES DEMON: HD 1; AC 5 [14]; Atk 2 claws (1d2), 1 bite (1d4); Move 5; Save 18; CL/XP 2/30; Special: Half damage from non-magic weapons.

ENDRAD, CLERIC LVL 11: HP 31; AC 2 [17]; Save 5 (3 vs. paralysis and poison); CL/XP 12/2000; Special: Banish undead, spells (4/4/4/3/3). Platemail, shield, mace, unholy symbol.

MEDUSA: HD 6; AC 5 [14]; Atk 1 weapon (1d4); Move 9; Save 11; CL/XP 8/800; Special: Gaze turns to stone, poison.

KARRAN, MAGIC-USER LVL 11: HP 30; AC 9 [10]; Save 5 (3 vs. spells); CL/XP 11/1700; Special: Spells (4/4/4/3/3). Staff, dagger, spellbook, pouch of very mild tobacco (1 lb, worth 20 gp).

0701 Haunted Vale:

A deep valley in the mountains here appears to be haunted. A gang of seven air mephitis uses their powers to cause an old coffin to rise up and spin around, all while making terrible shrieks and groans. Legend says that the evil spirit here can be propitiated by throwing an offering of wineskins into the vale.

0822 Two Faces of Evil:

Two Faces of Evil: A trail that runs south through this hex is guarded by a two-headed troll called Korog. Korog protects two caves set about 100 feet above him in the side of the mountain. Both are carved in the image of troll faces, one having a gaping mouth of fangs, the other a round mouth that "vomits" a rust-colored waterfall down the slope and into a pool that feeds a subterranean river that eventually flows into the river at [0620].

TWO-HEADED TROLL: HD 10; AC 3 [16]; Atk 2 weapons (1d10) or 2 claws (1d6); Move 12; Save 5; CL/XP 11/1700; Special: Rend with claws (2d6), regenerate 1 hp/round, surprised on 1 in 8.

[A] This chamber consists of two wide passages that meet in a circular chamber with a 30-ft high ceiling. There is a locked iron door on either end of the room. Flanking both doors there are bas-reliefs of trolls with open mouths. The floor of the circular chamber is clad in blocks of polished amber. The walls in the circular chamber are also polished very smooth. When the amber blocks are trod upon, the bas-reliefs emit powerful streams of scorching wind. These winds meet in the center and turn into a whirlwind (per the air elemental monster). The winds are so hot that they inflict 1d4 points of damage per round.

[B] The walls of this cross-shaped chamber are carved in bas-reliefs of bowing trolls. At the center of the chamber there is a pool that bubbles and spits, with each drop of liquid that hits the floor taking the form of a small insect and scurrying away towards a crack or crevice in the bas-reliefs. One can just make out, through the viscous, ochre-colored water in the pool a winding stair leading down to the bottom. At the bottom of the pool there is a 10-ft tall pocket of air. Moving through the waters is safe for trolls and other creatures that can regenerate damage. Other beings must pass a saving throw or be mutated by the water:

D20	Mutation
1–2	Forearm separates at elbow into two forearms (–1 to dexterity)
3–4	Foreleg splits into two forelegs (–1 to dexterity, –3 to movement)
5–6	Skin develops thick callouses (-1 [+1] to Armor Class)
7	Multiple muscle layers (+1 to Strength)
8	Shortened tendons (+3 to movement)
9	Redundant vital organs (+1 constitution)
10	Third leg (–1 dexterity, +3 movement)
11	Third arm underneath existing arm
12	Second head (+1 Intelligence; 50% chance it is chaotic)

All mutations that obviously alter the person's body reduce their charisma by 3 points. No ability modification can reduce an ability score below 3 or above 18. At the bottom of the room there is a locked iron door that vibrates and hums.

[C] This hexagonal room has a raised platform in its center. There are three triangular, phosphorescent stones set into the ground around the central platform. The walls of the central platform have phosphorescent hand prints on them (marked with arrows on the map). Ladders allow one to access the top of the platform. In the center of the platform there is a 3-ft wide pit lined with phosphorescent stone. A chain ending in a metal disc and attached to a winch allow people to be lowered easily into the pit. Once a person or animal is in the pit, the platform's magic can be activated by three magic-users touching their hands to the hand prints on the platform. This creates clones of the person or creature in the pit, which appear on the triangular stones. One of these clones is always lawful in alignment, and over-zealously so. Another is neutral and obsessed with one of three things: Food, gold or romance. The third is always chaotic and very sneaky. The chaotic clone wants to kill the original creature and destroy it.

[D] Climbing up to the "vomiting" mouth is highly dangerous. The rocks are slippery, and there is no way to enter the cavern (except perhaps by the use of a fly spell) that does not involve entering the falling water and pulling oneself up through the torrent into the cavern beyond. This requires one to roll 1d20 under their strength or dexterity score (player's choice). A failure indicates a plunge down the waterfall for 6d6 points of

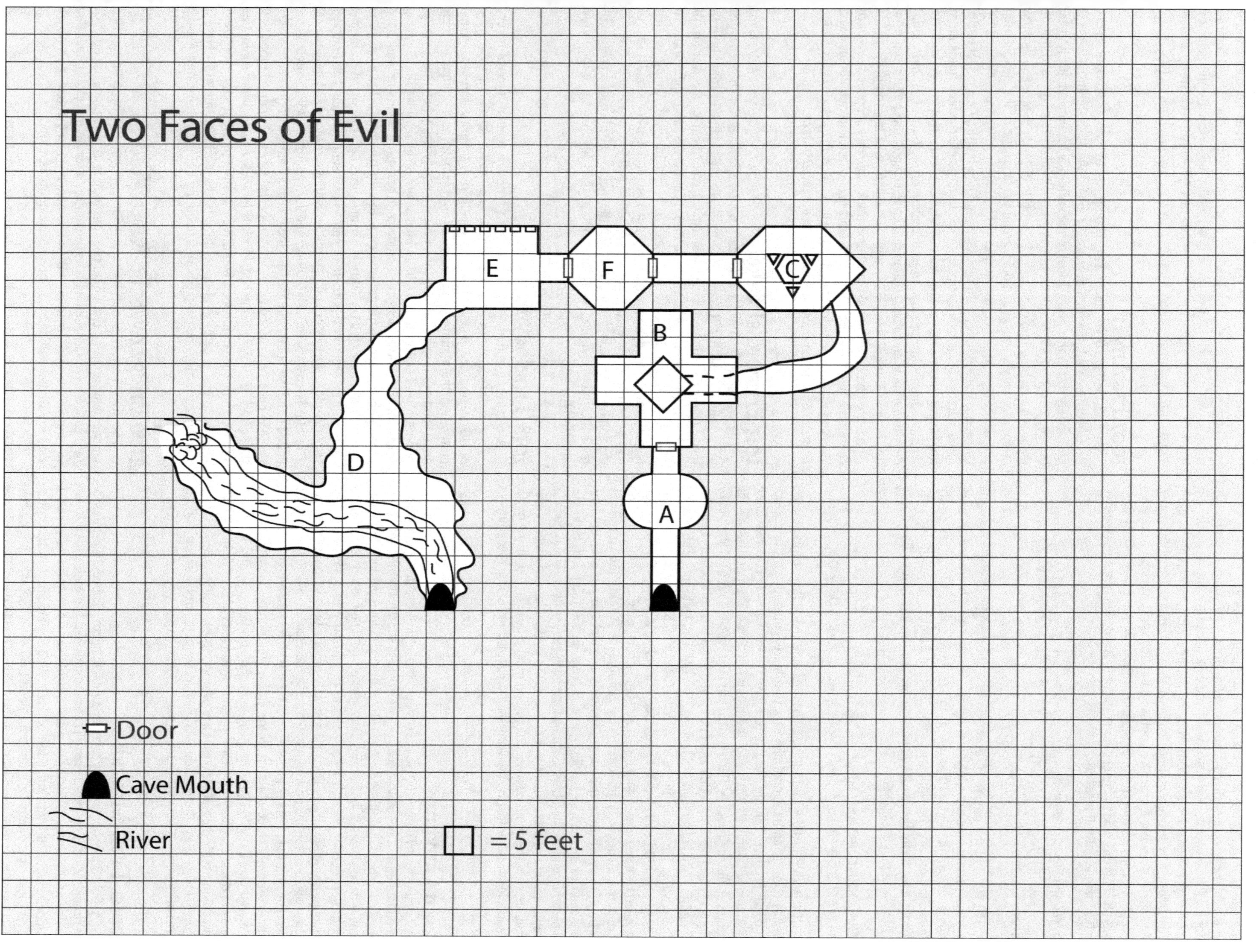

Two Faces of Evil
A
B
C
D
E
F
Door
Cave Mouth
River
= 5 feet

damage.

The cavern is Y-shaped and composed entirely of glass. A stream flows through it, originating at a second waterfall that plunges from a small crack in the cavern wall 20 feet above the floor. The room is unusually hot and steamy, and the glass walls are hot to the touch. A small, old red dragon named Ronodelis relaxes in the warm, soothing waters. His treasure is hidden behind the second waterfall in a shallow cave. Ronodelis does not appreciate company, but he is wily enough to engage people in conversation that he might lure them within range of his fiery breath. There is a 55% chance he is sleeping inside his treasure chamber when people enter the cavern.

RONODELIS: HD 9 (54 hp); AC 2 [17]; Atk 2 claws (1d8) and bite (3d10); Move 9 (F24); Save 6; CL/XP 11/1700; Special: Breathes fire.

[E] Beyond the cavern of glass, down a short flight of stairs, there is a long, rectangular room of glass bricks. On one wall there are six iron doors, not unlike those of an oven. Inside these doors, which are easily opened, there are the skeletons of malformed humanoids, each one with a ruby cast to its bones. If exposed to the air, these creatures flame into "life" as exploding bones.

EXPLODING BONES: HD 2; AC 8 [11]; Atk 1 weapon (1d8); Move 12; Save 16; CL/XP 3/60; Special: Explode when killed.

[F] Between the weird cloning chamber and the gallery of exploding bones there is an octagonal chamber that holds the study of the ancient wizard Frumm. Frumm was a weird old coot who discovered these abandoned chambers ages ago and moved in to work on perfecting the magical cloning process. Each wall of this room is covered with shelves of books, scrolls and the odds and ends that a great wizard collects over his long life. Two ladders, one 15 feet long, the other 30 feet long, lean against these walls. The books in the room are arcane in their scope, and each one (there are 300 in all) has a 1% chance of holding a piece of information needed by a researcher into the subjects of general magic, cloning, hybrid creatures, alchemy or the creation of homunculi. Attempting to remove a book or scroll from the room triggers a magical trap, as a thick chain attached to a manacle suddenly materializes on the thief's right ankle. The other end of the chain is embedded in the stone floor. If the book is replaced on the shelf where it was found, the chain dematerializes. Three rounds after the chain appears, the person must pass a saving throw or the manacle twists suddenly, breaking their ankle and inflicting 1d6 points of damage.

0901 Gundur:

Gundur is a village of 70 dwarves dug into a low, forested mountain in the manner of a beehive. Like most dwarves of the Troll Hills, they keep goats and bees, but these dwarves also cultivate fungal gardens in hidden caves. The dwarves have long since played out their silver mines here, and their deeply creased faces point to the quantity of lead they pulled out alongside the silver. They are now a dwindling population, as younger dwarves have left the community for the human settlements to the north to work as masons, miners and smiths. Those who remain are getting older; there are only three children in the entire community. The oldsters are veteran warriors (2 HD) who spend their days drinking, telling stories of the old days, carving little stone toys and ornaments and, once in a while, practicing with their weapons. They are very fond of tobacco, but have been cut off from the outside world since the petty trolls began making trouble.

0910 Troll Mound:

A field here holds many clay mounds that are shaped like piles of writhing arms, legs and heads. These mounds are something like totem poles to the trolls. If anointed with troll blood, a pile splits to reveal a sloped shaft that leads into a long cavern filled with charred troll corpses. The place is a dumping ground for dead troll shamans, who are burned by the trolls to lock their often vengeful spirits inside their bodies. These corpses retain a malevolent intelligence that burns and hates and infuses others with that hate, possessing them and turning them into berserkers (per *heroism* spell). A saving throw is permitted to avoid the hatred, but if failed the person flies into a foaming rage and attacks his fellows for 1d6 rounds. Within each corpse there is a bloodstone – actually the petrified heart of the troll shaman. Each bloodstone is worth 1d6x30 gp and is sought after by magic-users for use in their potions and researches.

1007 Fat Anya:

A ruined village of the ancient men composed of blue glass is spread out here over three hills, with a dry canal running between the hills. Several glass boats rest in this gully. Most of the buildings here are simple homes, but one larger building holds a library of books that are so dry and fragile that even touching one can turn it into a pile of dust (chance equals 80% minus dexterity score). The books are in the language of the ancient men and cover a wide variety of subjects. The library entrance is flanked by two statues of sphinxes with owl faces and lion bodies. One portal in the library gives access to a staircase to the library cellar, which holds more books and the lair of the hag called Fat Anya. Fat Anya is a rotund hag with pendulous breasts, a grimy, shapeless dress, blue-black hair, long, dirty finger nails and a face that is sunken in and porcine. Fat Anya is now dwelling at Little Rock [3311] with her sisters. She has trapped her lair with a fire glyph located inside a large, thick tome that is opened to a page containing diagrams explaining the workings of ancient man technology. The very next page holds the glyph, which, if read, explodes in a 5 dice fireball and sets the remaining books in the cellar ablaze.

1013 Primordial Lake:

The witchmen and trolls alike call this lake Mother, for the believe it to be source of all life. The gods, they say, formed man and animals from the clay on the shores of the lake. They baked them in the warmth of the newborn Sun and breathed life into them here, setting them loose to explore the world. The clay of the lake is, in fact, magical. Any figure that is well crafted in the image of another can be turned into a simulacrum of that person, without their memories or abilities. The clay must be dried in the sun over three days' time and then the maker must breath a portion of their life into the figure, sacrificing one of their levels to give the figure one Hit Dice.

1018 Troglodytes:

A narrow cave that spits out boiling vapor at a regular interval (every 125 minutes) leads to a series of limestone caves inhabited by a tribe of 40 troglodytes. The troglodytes dwell in the warm, humid caverns, cultivating their slimes and jellies (they seem to be immune to their acids) and raiding the surface for sweeter cuts of meat when they find the opportunity. The troglodytes have blue scales striped with bilious green. They carry a hodge-podge of crude and borrowed weapons and have hide shields. The caverns are littered with industrial grade diamonds (one could collect about 1d4 x 100 gp worth with a day's labor). The largest cavern in the complex is their temple. The back wall has been carved into a crude representation of a reptilian with a skull face and long claws. The idol is covered in dried blood and is worshipped by a witchdoctor called Cthothacho. Before the idol there is a sky sledge of the ancient men that has been repurposed as an altar. It is also covered in dried blood and the surface is heavily scratched, but it is in working condition. A reduced strength lightning bolt (one dice) directed at the machine can energize it for 1d4 hours. It can travel up to three hexes per hour, but will give out suddenly. Starting the device with a lightning bolt ruins it for future use.

1106 Bridge over the River Wide:

The river here is about 300 feet wide and spanned by a bridge that allows boats up to 30 feet tall to pass through. Lurking in the supports is a troll called Yovern. Bored with its life, it gladly leaves travelers unharmed in return for a story or song, unless it is hungry (1 in 6 chance), in which case it will demand a horse or two humanoids as a toll.

TROLL: HD 6+3; AC 4 [15]; Atk 2 claws (1d4), 1 bite (1d8);

Move 12; Save 11; CL/XP 8/800; Special: Regenerate 3 hp/round.

1203 Powwow:

Thirty golden men are having a powwow here around a trio of tall poles surmounted by busts of their gods of Life, Death and Time. Of the thirty men, five are powerful shamans among the golden men, the others are their retinues. Each shaman hails from a different tribe, most of them from the savannah beyond the mountains. Leather tents surround the powwow site. The three posts are 20 feet tall and about 3 feet in diameter. They are placed at the center of a flat mound about ten feet apart from one another. The shamans dance and chant around and through this assemblage of deific might, casting colored pebbles at the things and then, every so often, falling to their knees to read the stones for signs.

The poles do not tolerate the presence of strangers who have not been blessed by the shamans and anointed with the blood of a hawk (on their belly), dove (on their chest) and deer (on their forehead). The poles can animate and move as though made of rubber, clubbing people or grappling and constricting them. The heads atop the poles can swallow people, sending them to a chamber beneath the hill where a blue savant is imprisoned. The blue savant is a rotund man in a loincloth and poncho of cloth-of-silver. He looks to be a gap-jawed fool, with stark, white hands and a lolling white tongue. Despite his appearance, he is intelligent and cunning and can communicate with people by touching his fingers to their temple.

TOTEM POLE: HD 4 (17 hp); AC 5 [14]; Atk 1 slam (1d8); Move 0; Save 13; CL/XP 5/240; Special: Constrict (1d8), immune to mind effects.

BLUE SAVANT: HD 10 (53 hp); AC 8 [11]; Atk 1 strike (1d4 + disease); Move 12; Save 5; CL/XP 13/2300; Special: ESP, touch causes blue plague (save to negate), magic resistance (20%), immune to fire and electricity.

SHAMAN: HD 8 (41 hp); AC 9 [10]; Atk 1 (1d6 or weapon or spell); Move 12; Save 8; CL/XP 10/1400; Special: Shape change, cast spells as 8th level druid.

1220 Hecaton:

A hundred-handed horror lurks in the mountains. Spawned ages ago by the land to deal with the ancient men and their matrix, it was defeated by the blue savants and forced to retreat into the mountains to slumber. The horror is still weak from its exposure to the energies of the blue savants. The trolls regard him as their god of death, and leave offerings of prisoners and prey before his cave. The creature might awaken briefly to take these offerings, as it slowly regains its strength for a final assault on the humans of the Troll Hills.

HECATON: HD 20; AC 4 [15]; Atk 10 fists or weapons (5d6); Move 9; Save 3; CL/XP 24/5600; Special: Hurl boulders (as *meteor swarm*, range 75 feet), magic resistance (25%), stunning appearance.

1312 Jenny o' the Green:

Jenny o' the Green dwells just beyond a swiftly flowing stream crossed by a partially collapsed bridge. Jenny's lair is a domed building with thick, undulating columns and steps. Inside there is an ancient art gallery, the art all being damaged and smeared with filth. Gargoyles that look like men with long, tubular arms and legs and faces that suggest an nightmarish elephant lurk on a wide shelf that runs along the bottom of the dome, which is painted bright yellow. These five gargoyles serve Jenny, a hag with green skin, long legs, bony hips, long arms that drag on the ground when she walks and stark white hair that looks like a rat's nest. Jenny dwells in a pit she has dug in the floor of the gallery and lined with rushes and leaves. Inside her pit there is a wooden cabinet with ten drawers, each one locked (thieves can pick these with a +15% bonus). Each drawer (save one) holds a glass marble composed of swirling colors. These marbles cause a tingling sensation in one's finger tips. If thrown against a surface

and shattered, the marble causes a break down in physical laws per the following table:

Roll	Effect
1	Gravity in a 1d4 x 5 ft. radius is reversed
2	Time in a 1d3 x 5 ft. radius stops flowing for those within the radius (i.e. they are frozen) for 1d4 rounds.
3	Space rolls and cracks, switching the positions (randomly) of all creatures in a 1d2 x 10 ft. radius.

JENNY O' THE GREEN: HD 8 (27 hp); AC 1 [18]; Atk 2 claws (2d8) and bite (1d8); Move 12; Save 8; CL/XP 11/1700; Special: Hug and rend, polymorph, call mists, only harmed by +1 or better weapon.

1422 Fire Trolls:

In a charred cave, five fire trolls dance around pits of charcoal where fire leaps into the air. Slaves covered in soot tend these fires, which the trolls use to make troll-sized weapons – a valuable skill among creatures who normally cannot tolerate the touch of fire. These weapons are traded to other tribes by bands of petty trolls. The slaves cough and wheeze, and when they grow tired they fall into the fires and are roasted for the trolls' supper. The largest troll rules over his brothers, who resent him and would see him undone had they they courage to defy their mother, the hag Black Bess [1510]. He dwells in an adjacent cave scattered with ashes. Here, he keeps the clan treasure (12,630 sp, 5,390 gp and a large amber worth 800 gp) and his person treasure, an exotic dancing girl from the southern city-state of Crescentium. Her pale skin is now mottled with soot, her silver-blond hair streaked with ash, her eyes red from the acrid fumes and her own tears. She wears chains forged by the trolls and secured into the walls with iron spikes.

FIRE TROLL: HD 6+3; AC 4 [15]; Atk 2 claws (1d4 + 1d6 fire) and bite (1d8 + 1d6 fire); Move 12; Save 11; CL/XP 10/1400; Special: Fiery, regenerates 3 hp/rd (normal damage from acid and cold), immune to fire.

1503 Bear Goddess:

There is a valley here with gold-flecked stones, a pleasant, babbling stream and tall pine trees that keep is shrouded in a perpetual shade. The entrance to valley is blocked by a steel gate, the central bars of which are etched with warnings that this valley is sacred to the Bear Mother and not to be disturbed. The gate is not locked. About one mile past the gate there is a shrine on the east side of the brook. The shrine is made from pine and carved to represent tiny black bears dancing around a much larger bear – presumably the bear mother. An offering plate carved from hematite sits before the idols. It holds a few acorns and a bit of honeycomb. Another vessel, carved from stone and painted with wise bear faces holds cool holy water. A few moments after travelers enter the shrine or pass it, a wrinkled old man in a bearskin coat will appear on the road, a staff in his hands. The man has striking blue eyes and a mane of red hair that flows seamlessly into his beard. "This valley," he will proclaim, "is off limits. Turn back in peace." As he speaks these words, twelve black bears will make their presence known in the woods around the travelers. The man, Kromog, is a werebear, but his companions are not.

Further into the valley there is a massive cave – almost a natural amphitheater, but deeper – in which a massive idol of the Bear Goddess has been carved. Her priests, there are ten in all, are werebear druids who dwell in smaller caves located near this central temple. Offerings of food and flowers are made here, as well as ritual combats to drive away winter (in the form of a female warrior dressed in white) in the Spring. The werebears claim that the Bear Goddess lived here before the ancient men walked in the Troll Hills and will persist after their final extinction.

A secret door in their great temple located behind the bear idol's right eye leads into a complex of granite caves that delve deep into the earth. Here, the ancient priests and priestesses of the temple "hibernate" as mummies. Other strange things walk these caverns as well, including all manner of oozes and vermin and a few more powerful fey creatures that were driven into these caves by the ancient men and still harbor a deep hatred towards them.

The werebears of the valley fear the trolls and fight them constantly to preserve the valley, for the trolls represent nature in its most violent and frightening aspect. They also hate the ancient men, with whom they share blood, for their own ancient excesses. Of the witchmen and elves they know little, but their default position is one of disdain. The dwarves they know well. Dwarves sometimes come to the shrine to leave offerings of peace and ask the druids for help.

BLACK BEAR: HD 4+1 (18 hp); AC 7 [12]; Atk 2 claws (1d3) and bite (1d6); Move 9; Save 13; CL/XP 4/120; Special: Hug.

WEREBEAR DRUID LVL 3: HD 7+3 (36 hp); AC 2 [17]; Atk 2 claws (1d3) and bite (2d4); Move 9; Save 9 (7 vs. fire); CL/XP 9/1100; Special: Lycanthropy, spells (3/1).

KROMOG, WEREBEAR DRUID LVL 8: HD 8+3 (41 hp); AC 2 [17]; Atk 2 claws (1d3) and bite (2d4); Move 9; Save 8 (6 vs. fire); CL/XP 10/1400; Special: Lycanthropy, spells (4/3/2/1).

1507 City of Blue Glass:

When the energy matrix of the ancient men went critical, it turned everything within three miles - all the buildings of the city and the streets - into blue glass. The chemical make-up of the plant and animal life was also changed. Where normal plants derive their sustenance from the sunlight, the plants that surrounded the ancient city now drew their sustenance only from the ultraviolet rays of the Sun. The plants turned blue, the bark of the trees blue-black, the fruits a sort of purple. While the humans of the city disappeared, the lower orders of life persisted in an altered state. They were also turned every shade of blue, and could only draw sustenance from the blue plants that surrounded the city.

The strange blue city, once called Thett, is now occupied by animals (many deer, a few bears and many smaller creatures), the few humanoids and monsters that have succumbed to the blue plague and made it into the ruin before they starved to death and the remaining blue savants. The buildings of the city are largely intact, the glass walls usually being too thick to shatter or wear down easily. The streets are overgrown with blue grasses, weeds and vines. Most of the buildings have been well plundered, but there are many that still hold treasures of the ancient men – silver suits as light as cotton but as tough as mail, weird sledges that supposedly can be made to fly with the proper spells, etc. Glass tubes link the upper stories of these buildings. One building in particular, a great dome, holds many mysteries in its depths, not the least of which is the fabled matrix that still glows with a wan, blue light. If united with the crystal sword in [3111], the matrix can once again produce energy as it did, returning the city and land to normal.

1510 Black Bess:

Black Bess is a green hag remarkable for her very dark green skin and golden hair. She dwells in a crooked tree overlooking a mucky bog rife with poisonous fumes that turn one's skin black and pull the lips back from the teeth (lose 1d4 point of charisma per day unless a saving throw is made). She keeps her treasure, 710 sp, 130 gp, a chrysoberyl worth 60 gp and a pearl worth 100 gp worn as a stud in her nose, in various hollow trees in the area. Black Bess spawned the trolls in [1422].

BLACK BESS: HD 7 (35 hp); AC 1 [18]; Atk 2 claws (1d8) and bite (1d6); Move 15; Save 9; CL/XP 10/1400; Special: Rend with claws (two successful claw attacks, extra 2d6 rounds), fog cloud 3/day, magic resistance (10%), alter appearance to look like a maiden.

1702 Osgilt:

Osgilt is a village of about 100 dwarves situated in a vale of hickories. The dwarves live in a ring of dwarf-made mounds that are connected underground by tunnels and also connect to their mines, from which they dig iron ore. The dwarves process some of this ore about two miles away from their village on a slope in clay ovens. They trade the rest of the iron to the ancient men. While the dwarf men work in the mines below, their wives and daughters keep bees, raise goats and tend a garden small, hidden gardens near the village. The honey is used to made a delicious, though quite potent, mead and the dwarf women also know the secret of making dwarven moonshine. They usually have a dozen or so jugs of mead and one or two jugs of moonshine on hand for trade or celebration. The dwarves all dwell in separate mounds in family units – usually a patriarch and matriarch and their two or three children and maybe a dozen grandchildren. Quarters are tight, and not an inch is wasted. Men and women always have a hand axe on their person, and the men keep a crossbow, armor and shield handy. Mine entrances are always within these mound chambers, as each family has their own personal mine radiating out from the village. A stone tetrahedron – their understanding of God – hangs above these entrances from a golden string.

1711 Injured Elf:

An elf hides in a tree top, having escaped an encounter with several trolls with a broken leg. The elf, Archest, is a strapping example of the northern breed, with porcelain skin, curly, auburn hair and violet eyes. He wears a tarnished ringmail hauberk and has a longbow hanging from an iron spike driven into the tree. Half of a longsword rests in his scabbard and a silver trumpet is hangs from a leather belt around his neck. Archest has so far dealt with his injury by wrapping it in the remains of his cloak and by drinking liberally of three clay bottles of dwarven mead. He is mildly drunk (-2 to hit in combat) and desperate for help.

ARCHEST, ELF THIEF LVL 6: HP 17; AC 7 [12]; Save 11 (9 vs. devices); CL/XP 5/240; Special: Back stab x3, climb walls 90%, delicate tasks 35%, hear sounds 4 in 6, hide in shadows 30%, move silently 40%, open locks 30%, read languages, read magic writings. Leather armor, short sword, slings, 10 bullets, thieves' tools.

1714 Peggy Blackteeth:

Peggy Blackteeth is a mountain hag shaped like an ogress with black teeth and burnished, crimson skin. Her hair is stark white and stretches down to her ankles in long braids. Peggy Blackteeth spawned the petty trolls from [3014] and now dwells at Little Rock [3311] with her sisters, Mollie Longshanks [2421] and Fat Anya [1007]. Her cave is situated about 10 feet above the floor of a little valley strewn with boulders and covered by patches of poisonous blue mold. The cave is littered with bones and protected by a scything blade trap that strikes any who attempt to climb into the cave and disturb a few loose stones. Two starving women, twins about 20 years old, have been left in her cave, chained to opposite walls. Weird objects made from twigs and spider webs hang above them, intended to capture their spirits when they pass away.

1805 Crystal Temple:

There is a temple here that is constructed of blue, cubical crystals that measure 3 feet x 3 feet x 3 feet. The temple is conical in shape, as though meant to represent a mountain. There is a single entrance to the temple, a simple doorway shrouded by a curtain of blue beads. The interior of the temple, which measures 100 feet in diameter at the base and rises 300 feet in height, is like a cavernous space bathed in blue light. A 200-ft tall idol of Pokoth, the ancient men's goddess of death, stands in the center of the temple. Pokoth is tall and painfully thin, with an ape-like head and beady black eyes. Her skin is gray and she is naked. Nine crystal sculptures of gaunt, dancing women with their mouths and eyes sewn up surround the idol and can animate and attack if the idol or her priests are disturbed. The priests also number nine, with each one promised to one of the nine statues, which are meant to symbolize diseases, who re Pokoth's nine daughters. The nine priests are led by a high priest of the ancient, golden stock, a man named Darrimon, who is promised to Pokoth herself. Darrimon is a dashing young man who seeks to end the world by releasing Hecaton [1220]. He knows Hecaton favors the trolls, and goads him by taking their heads and preserving them. The heads hang from chains draped over the six arms of Pokoth's idol. Their bodies are interred below the temple.

Hidden shafts lead down to the these catacombs, which are crawling with headless trolls attempting to get back to their heads. Darrimon believes he needs 100 troll heads, and has thirteen left to go. He and his priests wear bone armor and carry steel maces and slings.

DEATH PRIEST, CLERIC LVL 1: HP 3; AC 4 [15]; Save 15 (13 vs. paralysis and poison); CL/XP B/10; Special: Banish undead. Chainmail, shield, mace, unholy symbol.

DARRIMON, CLERIC LVL 11: HP 43; AC 2 [17]; Save 5 (3 vs. paralysis and poison); CL/XP 12/2000; Special: Banish undead, spells (4/4/4/3/3). Platemail, shield, mace, holy symbol.

1821 Troll Cave:

Nine cave trolls, sons of Fat Anya [1007] dwell here in a high cave the overlooks a rock-strewn slope that ends in a cliff overlooking the foaming river. The trolls mostly live in edible fungi and what animals they can run down in the mountains. Despite being fairly stupid, they have managed to rig a trap that creates a landslide when a rope hidden among the rocks is tripped. Those on the slope suffer 2d6 points of damage and must pass a saving throw or be knocked into the river for another 1d6 points of falling damage. Keeping one's head above the roiling waters requires an open doors check each round. Each failure inflicts 1d6 points of damage and carries people 30 feet down the river. The trolls have a treasure of 4,890 sp, 2,750 gp, an aquamarine woth 50 gp and a wide silver basin filled with a weird, black substance that appears to be as much water as it is vapor. If a bit of a person's clothing or body (hair, blood, tooth) is dropped in the basin, a spectral troll climbs out and hunts that person down, returning them to the owner of the basin.

CAVE TROLL: HD 4; AC 0 [19]; Atk 2 claws (1d4) and bite (1d4); Move 24; Save 13; CL/XP 7/600; Special: Rend with claws (2d4), regenerate 2 hp/rd, *haste, spider climb*.

SPECTRAL TROLL: HD 6; AC 7 [12]; Atk 1 incorporeal bite (1d8) and 2 claws (1d6); Move 12 (F12); Save 11; CL/XP 9/1100; Special: Incorporeal (only harmed by magic weapons or spells, ignore physical damage 50% of the time), killed victim rises as spectre in 1d3 days, regenerate 2 hp/round, destroyed spirit reforms in 2d4 days unless basin is destroyed, vanishes in direct sunlight.

1908 Goblins:

A tribe of 240 goblins dwell here in the oozing mud of the river bank. The goblins are active in the spring and summer, but by late fall they burrow into the mud to hibernate, heal and regenerate. While active, the goblins range over the whole territory, feeding their voracious appetites with anything short of stones. They patrol in small gangs of 2d6+6 and are encountered in this hex on a roll of 1-3 on 1d6. Once prey is sighted, they begin hooting and hollering, attracting another pack of goblins 10% of the time. The goblins hide their treasure in chests about three feet beneath the mud. They have an unerring ability to find their treasures, but others have only a 1 in 20 chance per hour of searching to come up with anything.

2002 Old Griet:

Old Griet dwells behind a winding, narrow cavern that appears to emerge on a sunny meadow atop a butte. This is an illusion. The meadow has tall, waving grasses and cheerful yellow flowers. A maiden in plate armor sits in the grasses, surrounded by a coterie of nymphs with golden hair wearing chains of flowers. The maiden in armor is actually the hag called Old Griet, a manipulative old crone with a snaggle tooth, long, round nose, lank black hair and skin that blends with her surroundings. Her "nymphs" are clay men who long to turn into adventurers and see the world. The illusion is not a product of Old Griet, but rather of a powdery white mold that covers the tunnels that lead to the large, subterranean vault that people believe is a sunlit meadow. Old Griet delights in charming young men and sending adventurers to hassle her sisters.

OLD GRIET: HD 7; AC 4[15]; Atk 2 claws (1d6 + dexterity drain), 1 bite (1d8); Move 12; Save 11; CL/XP 7/600; Special: Chameleon skin (surprise on 3 in 6), touch drains 1 point of dexterity that returns in 24 hours.

2017 Invisible Man:

Nine moaning devilkins are huddled here in the shade of an overhanging cliff. They mew and moan and move swiftly to intercept travelers in the narrows below. The stone shelf they perch on contains the invisible body of a man, preserved after death in a silver suit. He sleeps the sleep eternal, caused by the ingestion of a poison delivered by a rival. The man, Zathr, was a technician of the ancient men from the time before their fall. He has blazing red hair and soft eyes of blue. If awakened, he will find it difficult to cope with the passage of years and destruction of his people.

MOANING DEVILKIN: HD 2; AC 1 [18]; Atk 1 tail-barb (1d4); Move 3 (F12); Save 16; CL/XP 4/120; Special: Moan.

ZATHR: HD 1d6 (2 hp); AC 9 [10]; Atk 1 strike (1d3); Move 12; Save 18; CL/XP B/10; Special: None.

2201 Rhost:

Rhost is a dwarf trading village with a population of 130 dwarves. The dwarves here have constructed a stone shell keep reminiscent of the style of their normal mound villages. Where most dwarves live in loose communities of families, the dwarves of Rhost have an elected mayor named Garond. Garond is a master mason and, more importantly, a canny trader and skilled politician. He plays the simple rustic, but his people know well not to underestimate him. Most of the dwarves of Rhost are artisans and soldiers. Rhost has no miners, but plenty of goatherds and farmers. Like other dwarves, they grow their crops in secluded groves away from their village.

2213 Trolls:

Eight trolls dwell in caves set into the side of a green hill. A human skeleton hangs over the entrance to the place, a copper bracelet worth 20 gp on its right arm. This is a trap that, if sprung by pulling on the bracelet (which is wired to the wrist), causes heavy stone to shower down on the people, effectively sealing the cave. The rock can be cleared in about 20 man-hours of work (about 20 troll-turns).

Beyond the entry tunnel there is a long gallery that shows signs of being carved by human hands. It is dusty and reeks of troll-stink. At either end there are stairs leading down into the living quarters of the trolls and deeper, cooler caves used to hold their meat and drink. The largest living quarters are possessed by the largest troll, a bruiser named Domno, who has a perpetually sneering lip and a nose so bulbous and warty one might think a morning-star had been attached to his face. Domno holds two shivering witchwoman slaves clad in soiled furs and nearly blind they've been underground so long. They are Domno's cupbearers. One, Alva, still resists the troll as subtly as she can, while the other, Sophelia, has had her spirit broken and now calls the troll her "big brother".

A large, oak door in Domno's chamber leads into a circular ritual chamber. The oak door is not only locked, it is barricaded by stone. Inside, the room is a perfect hemisphere, with polished white walls and floor. A seven-pointed star is worked into the floor in silver (worth 100 gp if removed). Touching the silver causes it to glow, with each point a different color. The colors project onto the walls in shimmering splendor, and soon begin to rotate, creating a *prismatic spray* effect. After ten minutes, the colors coalesce in the center of the star into a sphere of roiling colors. The sphere speaks in a booming voice, asking "What knowledge do you seek?" The sphere will answer a single question per the *contact higher plane* spell. Touching the sphere causes a person to *polymorph* into a serpentine creature of light whose touch has the effect of one color of the *prismatic spray*. The serpent will attack all within the room and then burrow into the floor, never to be seen again.

TROLL: HD 6+3; AC 4 [15]; Atk 2 claws (1d4), 1 bite (1d8); Move 12; Save 11; CL/XP 8/800; Special: Regenerate 3 hp/round.

DOMNO: HD 9+3 (48 hp); AC 4 [15]; Atk 2 claws (1d6), 1 bite (1d10); Move 12; Save 7; CL/XP 11/1700; Special: Regenerate 3 hp/round.

ALVA, WITCHWOMAN FIGHTER LVL 2/ MAGIC-USER LVL 1: HP 13; AC 9 [10]; Save 13; CL/XP 2/30, Special: Darkvision 60 ft., find secret door on 4 in 6, immune to paralysis from ghouls, multiple attacks, parry, spells (1). Longsword, dagger, spellbook.

PRISMATIC SERPENT: HD 6; AC 5[14]; Atk 1 bite (1d3), 1 constrict (2d4); Move 10; Save 11; CL/XP 7/600; Special: Constrict, breath weapon (random effect, roll 1d6).

Roll	Color	Effect
1	Red	2d6 fire damage
2	Orange	2d6 acid damage
3	Yellow	2d6 electricity damage
4	Green	Poison (save or die)
5	Blue	Petrification
6	Indigo	Confusion (save to negate)

2308 Old Fortress:

An old stone fort overlooks the river here, its flared towers once commanding the river with large cannon. The cannon are long since removed, but the fort still stands here in good shape. Its primary inhabitants are three mimic trolls, who dwell in three of the four towers in the filth and decay common to troll lairs. The fourth tower, the living tower as they call it, houses a large trapper on the bottom floor and a colony of twenty giant bats on its upper floor, which is shrouded by a permanent darkness effect. A mimic that still takes the form of a large cabinet dwells in this darkness, feeding on the bats that grow too old to avoid it. Hidden in this darkness there is a *golden gauntlet* (worth 100 gp) that can be used to create darkness 30-ft radius effect or a blazing sphere of light once per day by making a fist and speaking the words "tile" or "krad".

The mimic trolls, Wilke, Staard and Fanth, despise one another, and one will almost certainly not come to his brother's aid until it is too late that he might enjoy his brother's death and strike his killers down when they are at their weakest. All three keep slaves taken by the petty trolls of Little Rock [3311], using them for menial labor and as a food source in the winter. All have broken, twisted ankles and have heavy chains running from collars to their hands and feet. Among them, in the tower of Fanth, there is an old fighting-man called Connard, a Xanlo river man.

Connard is slowly loosening the stones in his slave pit. This will open into a secret passage that run under the fortress and out into the hills. Ancient foodstuffs, all dried out or rotted away, fill barrels and casks in this tunnel, and there are about twenty of the strange pellet projectors favored by the ancient men. All of the projectors (treat as a heavy crossbow that is usable one handed and inflicts 2d6 points of damage) need to be cleaned and oiled to make them operable. There is a supply of about 300 rounds of ammunition for these weapons, and each pellet has a 1 in 6 chance of not working. Twenty pellets can be loaded into a projector's magazine at a time. A gray ooze lurks in this secret passage, feeding on rats and other vermin.

MIMIC TROLL: HD 9; AC 0 [19]; Atk 2 claws (1d8); Move 12; Save 7; CL/XP 11/1700; Special: Assimilate magic, regenerate 3 hp/rd (normal damage from fire).

GRAY OOZE: HD 3; AC 8 [11]; Atk 1 strike (2d6); Move 1; Save 14; CL/XP 5/240; Special: Acid, immune to spells, heat, cold, and blunt weapons.

TRAPPER BEAST: HD 10 (36 hp); AC 3 [16]; Atk 1 enfold; Move 1; Save 5; CL/XP 11/1700; Special: Enfold and suffocate prey.

OLD MIMIC: HD 7 (30 hp); AC 6 [13]; Atk 1 smash (2d6); Move 2; Save 9; CL/XP 8/800; Special: Mimicry, glue.

2404 Troll Mines:

A gang of five gregarious trolls has set up a nice little operation in the woods around an old clay pit. Slaves are kept in the pit, slaves who burrow into the clay to retrieve blue kyanites. The trolls decorate themselves with these stones, making tiny slits in their flesh, inserting the stone and then permitting the flesh to rapidly heal around it. The trolls dwell in a cave overlooking the pit, and always have two trolls in the pit with the slaves and another troll standing guard above. The troll cave has a wide-mouthed entrance that leads to a downward sloping gallery with wide shelves. These shelves are where the trolls keep their sleeping furs and a few odds and ends (bowls, pestles, etc) carved from stone. Large wooden clubs are common. A higher cave is home to the trolls' pets, three black bears. A lower cave has a small pond fed by water dripping from the ceiling. Various stores, including casks of mead and wine, are kept here. The trolls also have a locked iron chest containing 5,100 sp, 1,800 gp and a kyanite worth 800 gp. The chest is trapped with poisonous gas. There are 1d20+15 slaves, most of them witchmen and Xanlo river men. They are bedraggled, and many of them show signs of twisted or broken limbs. They all wear soiled furs, fire not being permitted in the presence of the trolls.

TROLL: HD 6+3; AC 4 [15]; Atk 2 claws (1d4), 1 bite (1d8); Move 12; Save 11; CL/XP 8/800; Special: Regenerate 3 hp/round.

2411 Halflings:

A sloping meadow of sweet grasses and yellow flowers rests very near the river. A dozen burrows belonging to thirty halflings (half fey, half rabbit) are situated around a small rise strewn with white rocks. The halflings hold their community meetings on the mound, passing around an old *wand of protection from trolls* carved from oak with a tip shaped like an acorn from halfling to halfling to designate the permitted speaker. The halflings store roots like carrots and turnips in their burrows, which they use to make tarts that are sometimes infused with magic courtesy their wise woman, Calie. The halflings have a small treasure of finely carved furniture and some silver and gold ornaments worth a total of 500 gp, but probably weighing about 1,000 pounds.

HALFLING: HD 1d6; AC 4 [15]; Atk 1 short bow (1d6) or short sword (1d6); Move 6; Save 18; CL/XP B/10; Special: None.

CALIE, HALFLING DRUID LVL 4: HP 17; AC 7 [12]; Save 12 (10 vs. fire); CL/XP 4/120; Special: Spells (3/1/1), first mysteries leap. Leather armor, staff, holy symbol (lucky goblin's foot).

2421 Mollie Longshanks:

Mollie is a haggard mountain hag with skin the color of coal and hair as black as night. Only her white eyes, iron claws and iron teeth are visible in the night, when she prefers to hunt. She dwells in a cave – really a crack in the mountainside – that smells of sulfur. The interior is split into several caves radiating from a central cave at different depths. Pools of acrid, acidic water can be found in all of these caves, and an acid weird dwells in the deepest cave. The highest cave is home to Mollie, who collects eyes in glass jars filled with her own urine. The floor of her cave is covered in mouldering rushes that hide 2d4 giant rats, who serve her loyally. Mollie has left her cave for Little Rock [3311], joining her sisters and their collective spawn of petty trolls.

ACID WEIRD: HD 8; AC 5 [14]; Atk 1 bite (1d8); Move S12; Save 8; CL/XP 8/800; Special: Transparent (invisible until it attacks), reforms 1d4 rounds after "death".

2607 Swamp Trolls:

Fifteen swamp trolls, the sons of Mother Rawbones [2703], dwell here in a partially submerged house of gray bricks with a severely peaked roof – a style once favored by the ancient men. A round window of stained glass that depicts a weird face hidden among marigolds is set in the roof, allowing sunlight to filter through and casting weird shapes of light on the interior. The trolls hang their goods on wooden pegs pounded into the walls, including fur cloaks in dismal condition, leather satchels containing various items (knives, bone dice, rotting meat) and a large, round shield emblazoned with a purple moth. An iron nail in one wall can be pushed in to open a trapdoor beneath the murky waters. It leads to a submerged cellar holding casks and barrels that once contained ale and salted fish. There is also a large copper box sealed with wax. The box is locked and contains the body of an ancient woman in suspended animation. The woman, Telyth, was a murderess who was hidden in the box by the man who ran this tavern. How she came to be preserved is unknown, though the box radiates a weird, crimson magic that no magic-user can quite identify. Telyth lies in a fetal position. She wears a leather cat suit and has three hidden daggers on her person.

SWAMP TROLLS: HD 3; AC 3 [16]; Atk 2 claws (1d6) and bite (1d8); Move 12; Save 14; CL/XP 3/60; Special: Swamp dependent, surprise (2 in 6).

TELYTH, ASSASSIN LVL 7: HP 26; AC 7 [12]; Save 9; CL/XP 6/400; Special: Disguise, poison, backstab x2, climb walls 89%, delicate tasks 35%, hear sounds 4 in 6, hide in shadows 30%, move silently 40%, open locks 30%. Leather armor, short sword, stiletto daggers (3, 1 is poisoned), vial of poison (save or die).

2703 Mother Rawbones:

Mother Rawbones is a painfully thin looking annis hag who dwells in a wicker and mud hut lodged in the branches of an old oak. The oak was split by lightning long ago, and so rises only about 10 feet tall before it forks. The hut reeks of sweat and other unpleasant odors and hung outside the hut are a number of glass flytraps of various colors and filled with sweetened water and several dead flies. These flies and other small insects form the diet of Mother Rawbones, who never eats humans or humanoids, but does delight in killing them and extracting their vital organs for her brews. Mother Rawbones' radiates a foul vapor that causes food brought within 10 feet of the hag to spoil. Potions spoil unless their owner passes a saving throw. A pile of oily furs hides her treasure of 1,300 sp, 1,300 gp, ten pounds of pine nuts and a jasper worth 5 gp.

Mother Rawbones spawned the trolls in [2607].

MOTHER RAWBONES: HD 8 (44 hp); AC 1 [18]; Atk 2 claws (2d8), 1 bite (1d8); Move 12; Save 8; CL/XP 11/1700; Special: Hug and rend, polymorph, call mists, spoil food.

2710 Clay Pit:

There is a deep pit with clay walls dug into the slope of a hill. The pit is about 15 feet deep and measures 50 feet wide and 30 feet deep. Dozens of humanoid shapes have been "cut" from the walls here, some man-sized, others troll-sized. The woods around the pit are haunted by several clay men. These figures are created by hags and used to make simple servants. Those that prove disloyal are left to linger in the woods alone. The clay men almost look like large, featureless gingerbread men. They are about 8 inches thick, but otherwise "two-dimensional". If a clay man manages to steal a person's possession they can take on a closer appearance to that person, duplicating their general shape but not their color. In this form, they possess half the person's class abilities and a crude set of their memories. If they steal a bit of a person (hair, finger nail, etc.) they can become a perfect double. Encounters with a clay man occur on a roll of 1-3 on 1d6 in this hex.

CLAY MEN: HD 4; AC 3 [16]; Atk 2 fists (1d6+1); Move 9; Save 13; CL/XP 5/240; Special: Immune to bludgeoning weapons, change shape slowly, move silently (65%), surprise on 1-3 on 1d6.

2713 Bodak Hollow:

This hollow, flanked by tall stands of oaks and hickory and blessed by a babbling stream, is home to a bodak. The bodak appears to be a moldering man devoid of hair save for a long, white beard. His skin is an unwholesome green color and his eyes are always closed, though he seems to peer directly into the eyes of others. The bodak was once an ancient man called Bruton, a scientist who found himself tempted by a beautiful woman and found himself at the center of the events that lead to the great cataclysm of the ancient men.

BODAK: HD 9 (37 hp); AC 0 [19]; Atk 1 strike (1d8); Move 9; Save 7; CL/XP 12/2000; Special: Only harmed by +1 or better weapons, immune to electricity, loathes sunlight (1 point of damage per round), gaze causes death (30-ft range, save at +2 or die and rise as bodak 24 hours later).

2805 Spectral Trolls:

Three spectral trolls dance around a frozen fire singing psalms to the "gods beyond the sky" who never answer but to yawn and curse. Mist swirls around them and becomes a whirlpool of black soil that threatens to suck material creatures deep into the ground to suffocate. The frozen fire speaks to people's souls, convincing them that the end is nigh and their worst fears are true. Shadows dwell within the fire and while people shutter and gasp at the thought of their worst fears being realized, creep from the fire to pull hope from them and kindle that flame.

SPECTRAL TROLL: HD 6; AC 7 [12]; Atk 1 incorporeal bite (1d8) and 2 claws (1d6); Move 12 (F12); Save 11; CL/XP 9/1100; Special: Incorporeal (only harmed by magic weapons or spells, ignore physical damage 50% of the time), killed victim rises as spectre in 1d3 days, regenerate 2 hp/round, destroyed spirit reforms in 2d4 days unless basin is destroyed, vanishes in direct sunlight.

2822 Crystal Sepulcher:

At the center of this hex is what appears to be a parkland that has fallen into disrepair. Hedges have grown wild, rose vines meander across chipped and cracked pavements, wooden cupolas have rotted away and statuary is overturned. At the center of this sylvan ruin is a sepulcher of blue glass, highly ornamented and topped with a glassy eyed angel holding a sphere that glints and gleams in the sunlight. The parkland is claimed by a gaggle of six trolls, who dwell in burrows far away from the sepulcher, which they fear as a place of permanent death.

The sepulcher has a glass door through which one can see, just barely, a coffin resting upon sculptured hands that seem to jut up from the ground. The door cannot be opened – the hinges no longer work – but it can be shattered with a blow from mace or hammer. The interior of the place is very cold, and seems to be coursing with static electricity that raises one's hair and causes painful shocks when one person touches another. The coffin holds the body of a woman, only 5'2" tall, in silvery robes.

The lid of the coffin can be lifted off. When this is done, the body turns out to be a beautiful maiden in the full flower of youth. The woman has pale skin and dark red lips. Her eyes, which slowly open, are brilliant green and her auburn locks reach to her knees. The maiden's name is Iavanie. She claims to have been the daughter of a blue savant who foresaw the destruction of the great city, Thett, and placed her in this magical coffin to preserve her. This is completely true, but the woman is not all she seems. She is a carrier of the blue plague but unaffected by it. More importantly, she is like a psychic beacon for the remaining blue savants that lurk in Thett and throughout the Troll Hills.

2917 Plague Bearers:

A party of six fur trappers dwells here in a log cabin half buried in the side of a hill. The trappers are Xanlo river men who have been stuck in the wilderness since the petty trolls made movement north dangerous. They are running low on supplies, and eight of their number has been lost to the blue plague (q.v.). The men have buried the bodies in shallow graves, and now fear to leave their cabin, for the last time they attempted to flee they were set upon by the risen corpses and lost two more of their friends.

One of the trappers, Huzbad, wears a ring of blue glass. This ring is the cause of the plague, and those who spend time around Huzbad must pass a saving throw each day to avoid contracting the blue plague. The trappers have 300 gp worth of furs and pelts and will gladly trade them for rescue. All of them are carriers of the blue plague, and each will come down with the symptoms in 1d6 days.

GHOUL: HD 2; AC 6 [13]; Atk 2 claws (1d3), 1 bite (1d4); Move 9; Save 16; CL/XP 3/60; Special: Immunities, paralyzing touch.

FUR TRAPPER: HD 1; AC 7 [12]; Atk 1 weapon (1d8); Move 12; Save 17; CL/XP 1/15; Special: None.

3002 Hunting Party:

A party of five elves in resplendent livery and gleaming platemail has ridden down from the north seeking the villain Archest, who stole the heart of an elf maiden as well as the silver trumpet of her father, Lord Cunobellis. The elf knights are Beriam, Cayce, Gondre, Gwiel and Seveen. All ride chargers and are armed with longswords, lances and longbows. Their retinue consists of a company of elf longbowmen on riding horses and a dozen cooshee to track down the scoundrel, who may be stuck in a tree in [1711].

COOSHEE: HD 3; AC 4 [15]; Atk 2 claws (1d4) and bite (1d8); Move 15; Save 14 (12 vs. charm); CL/XP 4/120; Special: Sprint, trip, surprise (3 in 6).

ELVES: HD 1+1; AC 5 [14]; Atk 1 sword (1d8) or 2 arrows (1d6); Move 12; Save 17; CL/XP 1/15; Special: None.

ELF KNIGHT: HD 4; AC 8 [11]; Atk 1 longsword (1d8); Move 12; Save 13 (11 vs. spells); CL/XP 5/240; Special: Cast spells as 4th level magic-user.

LADY SEVEEN, FIGHTER LVL 5/MAGIC-USER LVL 9: HP 25; AC 9 [10]; Save 10; CL/XP 7/600, Special: Multiple attacks, parry, spells (4/3/3/2/1). Mace, dagger, spellbook.

3014 Bluefort:

A tribe of 110 petty trolls, the sons of Peggy Blackteeth [1714] once occupied a sprawling castle of blue-gray stone set on a rugged hill. The bottom of the hill is a veritable swamp of tangled cypress trees. A stone causeway spans the bog, though it is overgrown with branches and vines that emit an acrid, ugly odor. The castle has a single wall 35 feet tall with circular towers 46 feet tall. The halls of the castle are now empty save for some tarnished suits of weird, angular plate armor and broken shields and weapons. The petty trolls of Bluefort have left for Little Rock [3311] to join their grandmother, Fat Anya [1007]. The dungeons of the castle have a secret trapdoor into ancient sardonyx mines that burrow into the hills. Weird oozes and vapors haunt these mines, and they are mostly played out, though a dwarf might find a fresh seam in the deepest portions. Strange music plays through the dungeons and disembodied voices of invisible spirits coo into people's ears and tickle the hairs on the back of their neck. The spirits serve a baobhan sith locked behind an iron door by the trolls and made to pluck a golden harp that has the power to *charm person*.

BAOBHAN SITH: HD 3; AC 9 [11]; Atk 1 slam (1d4) and bite (1d4); Move 15; Save 14; CL/XP 6/400; Special: Blood drain (only against enthralled, 1d4 damage), captivating dance (save or enthralled for 2d4 rounds), dying words (*curse*), spells (*ESP, plant growth, suggestion*).

3107 Sturdy Redoubt:

A sturdy redoubt of ivory colored stone has been built here overlooking the river. A ruin even in the time of the ancient men, it has a square footprint with four flared, diamond-shaped towers about 30 feet tall. The walls are about 30 feet tall as well. The towers have large, square ports barred by iron. The redoubt has a large courtyard overgrown with weeds and scrawny trees. A blockhouse in the middle holds shards of terracotta pottery that appear to have once been statues of women and beasts. The fortress was once held by 60 petty trolls spawned by Fat Anya [1007]. They have since abandoned the place for Little Rock [3311]. A flight of seven harpies has taken up residence in the courtyard trees.

HARPY: HD 3; AC 7 [12]; Atk 2 talons (1d3) and weapon (1d6); Move 6 (Fly 18); Save 14; CL/XP 4/120; Special: Flight, siren-song.

3III Five Statues:

There are five mystic statues in this hex, hidden among the oaks. Each one appears to be a smooth humanoid in white marble standing on a short pedestal that measures 10 feet in radius. You can roll randomly to determine which statue is discovered first. If a person steps upon a pedestal, a riddle appears to etch itself into the stone in that person's native script. By answering the ritual, the statue's outer skin shatters, revealing a glass sculpture within. This glass statue raises its arm and points to the next statue. The final statue points back to the first, which will now be holding a sword of glass that casts rainbows across the area when bathed in light. This sword is a *+2 longsword* that can project a prismatic sphere once per day. The now animated statue wields the blade expertly and must be defeated in combat to claim the prize.

STATUE 1 — *What devours words day and night, but learns nothing?* A: A bookworm

STATUE 2 — *As sharp as any spear, when I speak, warriors gather. What am I?* A: A horn

STATUE 3 — *I wrestle with maids and queens that I may feed their husbands. What am I?* A: Bread dough.

STATUE 4 — *I don't bite a man lest he bite me first, and bite me they do. What am I?* A: An onion or garlic

STATUE 5 — *My neck is curved, my spine straight and I sing from my sides. What am I?* A: A harp.

ANIMATED STATUE: HD 10 (60 hp); AC 1 [18]; Atk 1 longsword (1d8+2); Move 12; Save 5; CL/XP 11/1700; Special: Immune to poison, disease and mind effects, wields *+2 longsword*.

3I20 Headless Ghost:

There is a covered bridge here spanning a slow creek. The banks of the creek are clogged with reeds and pussy willows and the song of frogs fills the air. The bridge is haunted by the headless ghost of a man wearing leather armor and carrying a stout falchion. The man's head is kept in a jar in Mollie's Tower [0119]. If returned and buried before the bridge, the ghost fades away, leaving behind his *+1 falchion* that whistles in the presence of shape-changers.

HEADLESS GHOST: HD 8 (39 hp); AC 3 [16]; Atk 1 ghostly falchion (1d6+1 + decapitation); Move F15; Save 5; CL/XP 11/1700; Special: +1 or silver weapons to hit, falchion decapitates on a natural "to hit" roll of '20' (save negates, but damage doubled).

3223 Gin Mill:

An old witchwoman named Fanglyn dwells here with her three sons, Kaith, Swanan and Evelic. She claims to have lived here for 40 years, buying off the local trolls with her gin, made from juniper berries and considered the best from Xanlo to Crescentium. The woman and her sons dwell in an old gristmill made of weathered gray stone and situated next to a river. The old mill wheel still turns, though they've disconnected it from the millstone. The boys sleep downstairs on straw, their mother in the loft. Four oak casks of gin sit in one corner waiting for folks from down south or up north to make the trek inland and cart them away. A large, locked chest in Fanglyn's loft, hidden under a pile of quilts and other odds and ends holds 416 sp and 912 gp. There is also a small root cellar that holds baskets of juniper berries, dried or drying herbs, pickled roots and about a

dozen pixies trapped in jars and kept docile by the inclusion of marigolds, which act as a depressant on the fey. One wonders what Fanglyn has in store for the pixies.

FANGLYN'S SONS, WITCHMEN FIGHTER 4/MAGIC-USER LVL 2: HP 24; AC 9 [10]; Save 11; CL/XP 5/240, Special: Multiple attacks, parry, spells (2). Longsword, dagger, longbow, spellbook.

FANGLYN, WITCHWOMAN FIGHTER 4/MAGIC-USER LVL 8: HP 24; AC 9 [10]; Save 8 (6 vs. spells); CL/XP 6/400, Special: Multiple attacks, parry, spells (4/3/3/2). Longsword, dagger, longbow, spellbook.

33II Little Rock:

The "Little Rock" is the name given by the witchmen to a large promontory that overlooks the joining of the Great River and Sapphire River. Atop the rock there is a tower, constructed by the archimage Joaer the Jolly. The tower can only be entered by ascending through dungeons carved into the promontory, and these dungeons are now held by the petty trolls and the coven of hags that controls them.

The entrance to the dungeons is via a shallow river cave in the promontory. To open a secret door one must dive into the water and swim up under the secret door into a large, hidden cove. In the cove there is a large wench that opens the door. Three dead nixies have been impaled on barbed spears driven into the river bottom to discourage other nixies from messing about. The cove is large enough to hold three dragon-prowed longships (without sails) that the trolls use to attack shipping. The secret door is 20 feet tall and 15 feet wide.

The tower keep of Joaer is five stories tall and measures about 30 feet to a side. The roof is crenellated and features a dome of amber glass that illuminates the interior. All of the tower's rooms are constructed around the perimeter of a shaft that extends from floor to dome. Railed walkways allow one to move from room to room on a given level, but no stairs are provided to ascend or descend through the five floors. Joaer used levitation to move about, and there are hidden trapdoors in some of the rooms that were used by his acolytes. His guards dwelled in the dungeon. The tower is now inhabited by the coven of hags and is haunted by fragments of Joaer's psyche.

[A] This chamber is extremely cold. The floor is covered in one foot of slush and in the middle of the room there is a large statue of a frog. The statue is made of blue glass with veins of silver running through it. Anytime something moves in this chamber (and movement is reduced by half from the slush and the slippery floor beneath it), the eyes of the frog glow and send out a charge of electricity (3d6 damage to target, 1d6 damage to all within 5 feet) with perfect accuracy. Unfortunately, a creature that stands still in this room has the slush around their feet solidify into ice. This reduces their movement by 3. The ice continues to climb up their body while they remain in this room, dropping their movement rate by 1 each round and inflicting 1d4 points of damage.

[B] A giant bear is chained to the north wall of this room. The chain is long enough that it can range throughout the room and about five feet out the door.

BEAR: HD 8; AC 6 [13]; Atk 2 claws (1d8+1) and bite (2d6+1); Move 12; Save 8; CL/XP 8/800; Special: Hug.

[C] Beneath the secret trapdoor in the ceiling in this room there is a round, metal plate about four feet in diameter colored vivid green with an "X" emblazoned on it. Creatures that stand on the plate are magically held and will assume any body position shouted at them. This would be amusing save for the reality of the plate. The image atop the plate is an illusion. The actual creature that stands on the plate is shifted into a small, circular chamber colored the same vivid green in pocket dimension. This chamber is inhabited by a cockatrice that guards a treasure. The person does not return from the pocket dimension until they are ordered to assume an "X" shape (arms above heads, legs in a wide stance). The cockatrice's treasure includes three petrified robbers, 2,140 sp, 2,000 gp and a green,

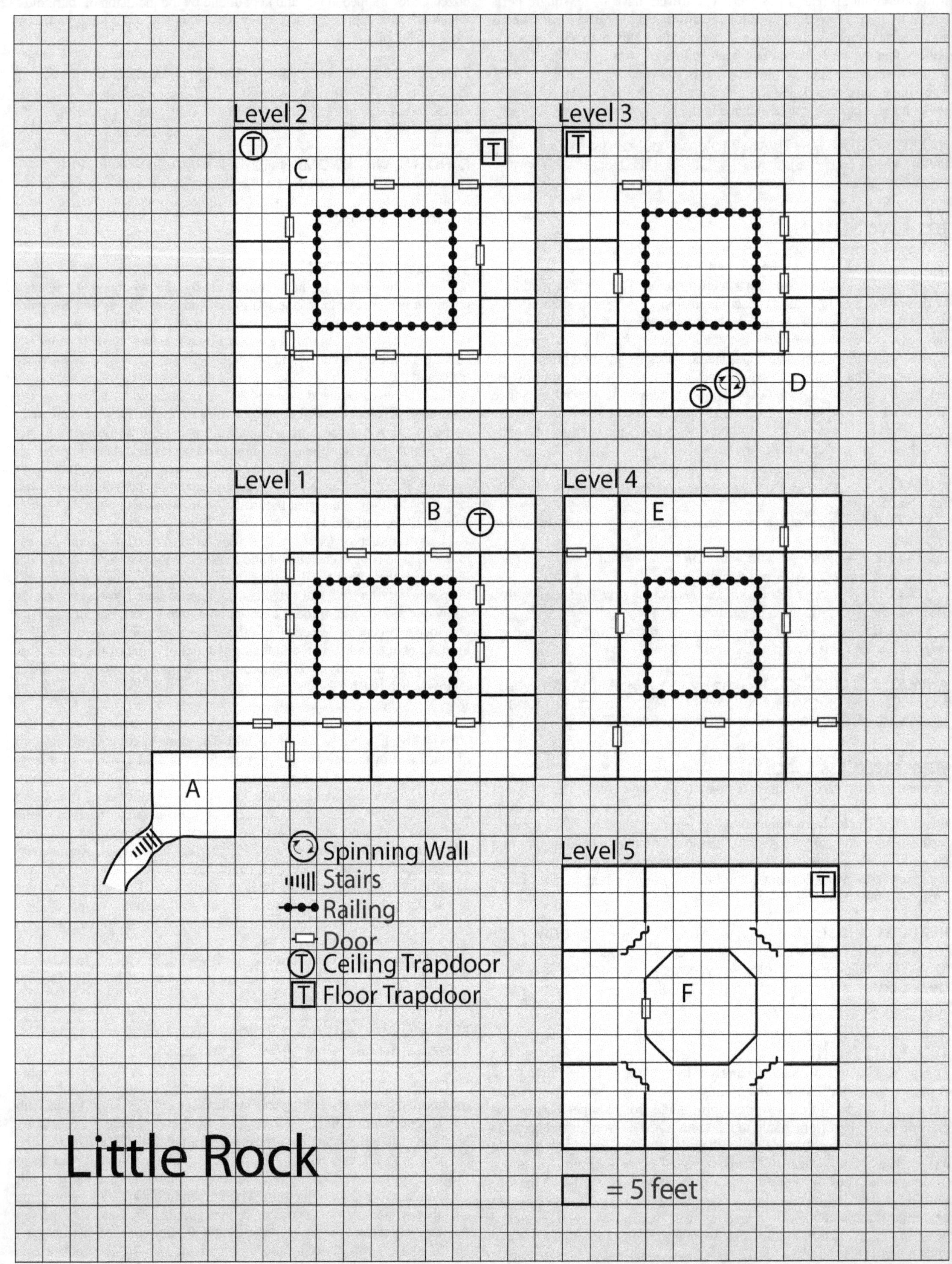

Level 2
C
Level 3
D
Level 1
B
Level 4
E
A
Spinning Wall
Stairs
Railing
Door
Ceiling Trapdoor
Floor Trapdoor
Level 5
F
= 5 feet
Little Rock

metallic rod that, when tapped against any surface returns the person to the room and frees them from the hold effect of the metal disc. The rod does not travel with them.

COCKATRICE: HD 5; AC 6 [13]; Atk 1 bite (1d3 + petrifaction); Move 6 (F18); Save 12; CL/XP 7/600; Special: bite turns to stone.

[D] This room is comfortably decorated, with thick rugs on the floor, oak paneled walls, numerous chairs and couches. One chair, a wooden, throne-like chair, is set against a wall. Anyone sitting on this chair causes the wall to rotate the person into the adjacent room, leaving an identical chair on the other side. The chair/wall trap is only one way; sitting on it in the room with the trapdoor does not make the wall rotate again. The only way the wall rotates is when somebody sits on the chair currently in [D]. Unfortunately, the chair has a secondary effect. Anyone sitting on it must pass a saving throw or have all of the metal they are holding turn to lead. This ruins magical items and makes metal armor four times as heavy and so soft that its armor value is reduced by half. The secondary effect is caused by a pressure plate on the chair that can be disabled by jamming a couple coins into the seams around it.

[E] This room is empty, with stained walls and a floor covered in grit. Its main inhabitant is a man with bluish skin. He wears dark, soiled clothes and has long hair that covers his face. Beneath that hair he has glassy eyes and a mouth that appears to have a lower lip but no upper lip – just tiny teeth peeking out from beneath a long nose. He is holding a puppy and sitting on the floor, rocking back and forth. The puppy is actually a figment of this blue savant's imagination, an imagination he can make manifest within a 30 feet radius. In effect, this works like any monster summoning spell, once per round. This blue savant walks with a limp. He has a key ring on his belt that opens many doors in the ruined blue city [1507].

BLUE SAVANT: HD 10 (51 hp); AC 7 [12]; Atk 1 strike (1d4 + disease); Move 9; Save 5; CL/XP 14/2600; Special: ESP, touch causes blue plague (save to negate), magic resistance (20%), immune to fire and electricity, imagination.

[F] This is the chamber of the three hags. They keep individual sleeping chambers behind the soiled curtains that block the outer rooms (except in the room with the trapdoor, where they maintain six petty trolls as guards. In their own chamber they keep a collection of mirrors and polished steel shields. Each one, when concentrated on by the hags, shows a different scene through a hag eye that has been placed somewhere important by their servants. One eye overlooks the witchman camp at [3722]. Others have been carried as far away as Crescentium and Xanlo. The hag treasure consists of 19,160 sp, 3,500 gp, a barrel holding 14 pounds of saffron (worth 15 gp per pound), a *potion of levitation* and a jump of unworked jade worth 105 gp.

PEGGY BLACKTEETH: HD 7 (42 hp); AC 4 [15]; Atk 2 claws (1d6), 1 bite (1d8); Move 12; Save 11; CL/XP 7/600; Special: Razor sharp claws do an additional 2d10 points of damage when she rolls a natural '20' to attack.

MOLLIE LONGSHANKS: HD 10 (38 hp); AC 1 [18]; Atk 2 claws (2d8), 1 bite (1d8); Move 24; Save 5; CL/XP 13/2300; Special: Hug and rend, polymorph, call mists, if wins initiative, attacks at beginning and end of combat round.

FAT ANYA: HD 8 (39 hp); AC 1 [18]; Atk 2 claws (2d8) and bite (1d8); Move 12; Save 8; CL/XP 10/1400; Special: Hug and rend, polymorph, call mists, half damage from weapons not forged of cold iron, no damage from wooden weapons.

3313 Wrecked Ship:

A keelboat has been driven ashore here by an attack from the petty trolls of Little Rock [3311]. The upper portions of the keelboat have been smashed, but the hull is still seaworthy. The only man to escape dragged himself into the bushes before he died. He wears sailor's garb and has a short sword gripped in his leathery hand. A pouch at his belt holds a brass compass, a love note from his wife in Xanlo and a plug of good tobacco. The ship carries four bales of cotton in the hold, with a single gold bar (worth 10 gp) hidden in one of the bales. A scrag lurks beneath the boat, waiting for curious adventurers to fall into his trap. The scrag descends from Black Bess [1510].

SCRAG: HD 6+3; AC 4 [15]; Atk 2 claws (1d4), 1 bite (1d8); Move 12; Save 11; CL/XP 8/800; Special: Regenerate 3 hp/round.

3418 Yellow Hoods:

The witchmen are given to collecting gods and philosophies as some people collect bottle caps. As each new idea passes before them, they conceive of its absolute brilliance and profess this brilliance to any who will listen. A few months or years pass and they have discovered some new scheme for ordering the universe. So it is with the Yellow Hoods, who have come to the Troll Hills to purify it of both trolls and men. As the universe must be destroyed that it may be made again, so the Troll Hills, the source of all life, must be purged of life that life may be recreated in a more perfect form (as defined by the Yellow Hoods).

The village houses 350 witchmen – an astounding number given how dangerous the Troll Hills are and the inland location of the village. Its safety is guaranteed by the presence of a powerful cabal, led by Quith, a devious little man with long fingers, a pleasant mustache and eyes that never seem to lock on to anything, but rather caress everything within sight, searching for the root and the weak spot.

The villagers are mostly farmers and shepherds. Their village consists of wood and brick buildings (the bricks are manufactured on site) clustered around a central square that contains a well. The well is carved to look as though a gray dragon curls around it. Stepping on the dragon's tongue releases the lock on a trapdoor disguised as a group of paving stones. The click is audible if there is complete silence, but the location of the paving stones is known only to the villagers. Beneath the trapdoor there is a series of galleries and catacombs filled with the boiled bones of hundreds of humanoids, from halfling to troll size. A simple stone altar provides a place for ritual killings, though most of the bones originated on hunts carried out by the cultists on horseback.

The cult numbers 30 individuals in all, including Quith's five lieutenants. When on the hunt or in their hidden temple they wear yellow robes and pointed hoods that cover their faces. They arm themselves with crossbows and long swords. Each cultist, when they join, has their left hand removed with the stroke of a sword while drinking a thick, black liquid. Within days, their hand regrows, but the flesh is as black as pitch and the touch of the hand drains one level or hit dice unless a saving throw is made at +3.

CULTIST (LVL 1): HD 1; AC 7 [12]; Atk 1 weapon (1d8); Move 12; Save 17; CL/XP 1/30; Special: None.

LIEUTENANT (LVL 3): HD 3; AC 7 [12]; Atk 1 weapon (1d8); Move 12; Save 14; CL/XP 4/120; Special: Magic-user spells (2).

QUITH, WITCHMAN FIGHTER LVL 4/MAGIC-USER LVL 6: HP 15; AC 9 [10]; Save 10 (8 vs. spells); CL/XP 5/240, Special: Multiple attacks, parry, spells (4/2/2). Longsword, dagger, crossbow, spellbook, vial of mercury.

3503 Shrine of Old Man River:

Old Man River is the name given to the spirit of the Great River, worshipped by the trolls and nixies who live in its waters, and by the river merchants and Xanlo river men who depend on it for their livelihoods. The shrine is a ghostly dome situated under the river, the top carved in the visage of an old man with a wild beard and head and unblinking eyes. One can enter the building via arched doorways on the north and south faces of the dome, doorways that look like that same bearded face, but with mouths stretched inhumanly to swallow up visitors.

Fortunately, one need not be able to breathe water to enter the shrine. Praying above the shrine in a boat and dropping a gift of seven silver coins wrapped in a parcel of white cloth tied by a black ribbon, calls the shrine to the surface with an explosion of bubbles. The shrine only remains above the water for one hour, so one must be quick to avoid the possibility of drowning. Inside the entrances one finds a narrow stairway that follows the curve of the dome and ends in a thick, bronze door covered with a layer of verdigris. The stairway from the north entrance goes clockwise while the other goes counterclockwise.

The doors open on a dome within a hemispherical chamber dominated by an idol of a muscular old man that appears to be made from water. The idol is, in fact, the genius loci of the river, a living mass of water that can assume any shape it likes. It stands in a pool of water about 15 feet in diameter and 10 feet deep, the pool being just another part of the creature. The creature stands 30 feet tall and is about 7 to 8 feet broad. Three small bull sharks swim within him.

There is only one priest of Old Man River, at least in this shrine, a nixie named Magda. Magda has been dominated by the creature, and allows it to access her intellect. Without a dominated subject, Old Man River has no intelligence of its own. The nixie's own repulsion at the sight of men and trolls has made the river angry with these creatures. When seven witchmen entered the temple to win the river over to their side, they discovered this wrath. They are now prisoners inside crystalline tubes that line the inner sanctum, tormented by the river and its priest. Six additional tubes remain empty. Within the pool of Old Man River there is an accumulated treasure of 14,100 gp and a golden flagon worth 800 gp.

OLD MAN RIVER: HD 35 (157 hp); AC 12 [8]; Atk 10 slams (4d6 + constrict); Move 3 (S3); Save 3; CL/XP 40/10400; Special: Enslave (save or completely under the control of the genius loci), when hit by a slam save or be constricted for 4d6 damage per round, regenerate 3 hp/round.

3514 Smuggler's Pit:

This hex contains a wooden trapdoor hidden beneath a covering of leaves and twigs. The trapdoor is situated next to an oak tree that has been split by lightning. The pit contains a variety of contraband. Roll 1d6 three times on the following table to determine the contents. There is a 3 in 6 chance that 1d8+6 smugglers are nearby.

Roll	Contraband
1	1d10 pounds of cloves (worth 15 gp per pound)
2	2d6 mink pelts (worth 10 gp each)
3	2d8 rolled cigars (worth 10 gp each)
4	3d6 pounds of silver (worth 1 gp per pound)
5	2d20 bear skins (worth 5 gp each)
6	2d20 pounds of pepper (worth 2 gp per pound)
7	1d12 wine barrels (30 gal. each, worth 10 gp each)
8	2d10 pounds of salt (worth 5 gp per pound)

SMUGGLERS: HD 1; AC 6 [13]; Atk 1 weapon (1d8); Move 12; Save 17; CL/XP 1/15; Special: None.

3606 Spawning Pool:

The Great River here forms a small pool of deep, green water that is used as a spawning pool for the local scrags. The scrags swim here in the spring to mate. The males then move back up or down the river, leaving the females to gestate and produce their voracious young. The petty trolls know to avoid this area in the summer months, as the young scrags, despite being less powerful than the adults, are more numerous and completely devoid of fear or reason. Encounters with 1d3 adult scrags occur on a roll of 1 on 1d6, while, during the summer months, encounters with 3d6 of the young scrags occurs on a roll of 2-3 on 1d6.

YOUNG SCRAG: HD 4+3; AC 4 [15]; Atk 2 claws (1d3), 1 bite (1d6); Move 12; Save 11; CL/XP 6/400; Special: Regenerate 3 hp/round.

SCRAG: HD 6+3; AC 4 [15]; Atk 2 claws (1d4), 1 bite (1d8); Move 12; Save 11; CL/XP 8/800; Special: Regenerate 3 hp/round.

3719 Farmstead:

A farmstead of 40 witchmen is situated here, growing crops in the rich river soil and raising a small herd of cattle. The farmstead is surrounded by an earthen rampart about four feet high and contains eight log longhouses and a large barn. The witchmen here are a rangy lot, the women wild eyed and disheveled, the men tall and slightly misshapen. Besides their cattle and crops, they raise wolfhounds and hunt in the woods with them. The unofficial leader of the village is an old woman Danasta, who some claim has made pacts with dark things in the woods, or maybe the trolls who dwell in the river. In either event, the Tevalar elves in [3816] leave them alone.

DANASTA, WITCHWOMAN FIGHTER LVL 4/ MAGIC-USER LVL 3: HP 4d8; AC 8 [11]; Save 11; CL/XP 4/120, Special: Multiple attacks, parry, spells (2/1). Longsword, hand axe, longbow.

3722 Witchmen Fort:

A small fort has been erected here in preparation of the witchmen making a final assault on the petty trolls of Little Rock [3311]. The fortress consists of packed earthen ramparts about 10 feet tall surmounted by 15-ft tall timber walls. There are two wooden guard towers, one situated on the northwest corner, the other on the southeast corner. Both towers provide a platform for up to ten soldiers to fire crossbows.

The fort was built mainly by the witchmen's zombie slaves, who have remained to form a company of brutish warriors. Besides the zombies, the fort is occupied by a company of crossbowmen in the russet and gold livery of Lord Tylias, a renowned scoundrel of Crescentium. Camped around the fortress there are three companies of archers, two companies of light infantry and one company of heavy infantry. In the nearby river there are seven galleys crewed by a 12 sailors and 60 oarsmen each.

The fort's commandant is Yoverus, a tall witchman with blistered skin, grey eyes and a mirthless face. He lounges in his office, barking orders to his subordinates and entertaining the other captains that have been assembled here. His office and quarters are in a wooden blockhouse. The fort also contains a zombie pit, barracks and combination armory and smithy. Yoverus keeps a locked chest containing 4,450 sp, 1,390 gp in his quarters, as well as three slave girls from the exotic tribe that inhabits the Floribunda peninsula far to the southeast. Yoverus decorates his room with ten panther skins (worth 15 gp each) and a barrel of 20 pounds of salt is kept in his chambers under lock and key.

Yoverus has no confidence in this attack, and plans on making a hasty retreat with a select band of troops and the fort's gold when the other troops have left for their attack.

ZOMBIE: HD 2; AC 8 [11]; Atk 1 weapon or strike (1d8); Move 6; Save 16; CL/XP 2/30; Special: Immune to sleep and charm.

WITCHMAN: HD 4; AC 3 [16]; Atk 1 weapon (1d8); Move 12; Save 13; CL./XP 5/240; Special: Can cast spells as 3rd level magic-user.

3803 Crazy Hermit:

There is a forge hidden here in the woods, though the plume of smoke that rises from it and the clanging of hammer on anvil makes it easy to locate on most days. The forge is run by a witchman named Gobeth, a burly man with a scruffy white beard and stringy white hair fringing his bald pate. Gobeth mutters to himself the most horrible curses while he works forging chains – though they are chains one cannot see unless they are enraged. When one looks upon the forge with eyes of anger and a thirst for vengeance, they see a great pile of red chains that hiss and spark while the man pounds upon them with his hammer. Gobeth lost his wife and sons to the trolls and his daughter to a prince among the Tevalar elves to the northeast. He can command the chains, which are not 100 feet long, and plans to use them to work his revenge on the prince. He will accept help on this journey, which is long and perilous, and will probably pass into the afterlife when his quest is finished, for the crimes committed against him happened 300 years ago, and surely he could not have lived that long.

GOBETH: HD 4 (12 hp); AC 9 [10]; Atk 1 hammer (1d4+2); Move 12; Save 13; CL/XP 5/240; Special: Cast spells as 2nd level magic-user. Leather apron, hammer, dagger.

3916 Trading Post:

The Tevalar elves, a tribe of aquatic elves from the flooded valleys to the northeast, has established a trading post here. The post looks like a tower rising from the river. There is a flooded outer wall that rises about five feet above the river and an inner tower that rises 12 feet above the water. The inner tower is used to store trade goods that would be ruined in the water. The outer wall houses the Tevalar merchants.

Within the inner tower one finds a random CL 3 treasure plus a number of mundane items from the basic equipment list, per the table below:

Value of Item	Percent Present	Number Present
Less than 1 sp	75%	1d6 x 10
1 sp to 9 sp	50%	2d6
1 gp to 10 gp	25%	1d8
11 gp to 100 gp	10%	1d4
100 gp +	5%	1

The Tevalar merchants wear loincloths of sodden cloth and belts of gold or silver (1d10x5 gp). They carry spears and three javelins each. There are usually two or three merchants present. For each merchant present, there are 1d4+2 human guards (amphibious due to the treatments of the elves) in the inner tower wearing mail and armed with crossbows and spears.

New Monsters

Devilkin

A few old adventurers have encountered the screaming devilkin, the most numerous of the devilkin, and told harrowing tales of them. Fewer have encountered their rarer kin in the Devil Peaks.

Cackling Devilkin

Cackling devilkins have faces twisted into masks of sorrow, with drooping, yellow eyes. They are smaller than screaming devilkins, but otherwise adhere to their body shapes. Cackling devilkins have warm, golden hides and bat wings of deep, lustrous russet. Their constant cackling goads people into a mad fury, forcing them to pass a saving throw each round or attack with whatever melee weapons they have on hand, including their bare hands. These attacks are made at a -2 penalty, but inflict +2 points of damage if successful.

CACKLING DEVILKIN: HD 3; AC 1 [18]; Atk 1 tail-barb (1d4); Move 3 (F12); Save 14; CL/XP 4/120; Special: Cackle.

Moaning Devilkin

Moaning devilkins have lavender scales, tiny, pinched faces with cavernous mouths and black wings. They are gaunt and long of limb, though their arms and legs are no more usable than those of other devilkins. They constant moaning is not only unnerving, but severely depressing. Those who hear it must pass a saving throw or fall into a funk, dropping their weapons and collapsing to the ground sobbing. After three rounds of sobbing, they must pass an additional saving throw or fall into a deep, dark sleep (per the spell).

MOANING DEVILKIN: HD 2; AC 1 [18]; Atk 1 tail-barb (1d4); Move 3 (F12); Save 16; CL/XP 4/120; Special: Moan.

Roaring Devilkin

Roaring devilkins have leonine faces atop long torsos. Their legs are squat and twisted while their arms are long and end in large, clawed hands. Bat wings decorate their backs. Their scaled bodies are a deep violet, lightening to blue around their mouths. Where screaming devilkins howl constantly, roaring devilkins save their existential pain for thunderous roars. They can do this once every three rounds. This roar causes 1d6 points of damage and forces one to save vs. deafening.

ROARING DEVILKIN: HD 4; AC 1 [18]; Atk 2 claws (1d3); Move 3 (F12); Save 13; CL/XP 5/240; Special: Roar.

Dinosaur - Ornithomimus

A few old adventurers have encountered the screaming devilkin, the most numerous of the devilkin, and told harrowing tales of them. Fewer have encountered their rarer kin in the Devil Peaks.

The ornithomimus was a bipedal, ostrich-like dinosaur with long legs and forelimbs and a thin, long neck. They have toothless beaks and are generally inoffensive omnivores.

ORNITHOMIMUS: HD 3; AC 7 [12]; Atk 1 bite (1d6); Move 18; Save 14; CL/XP 3/60; Special: None.

Petty Trolls

Petty trolls are seven-foot-tall trolls with dusky green skin, prominent noses and large ears decorated with studs and rings. The flesh inside their mouths is bluish green and their teeth are yellow. Petty trolls wear chainmail haubergeons and carry battle axes and longbows. They are a warlike people and more clannish than normal trolls, operating in groups of 2d6 x 10. Clans are led by powerful warchiefs with

PETTY TROLL: HD 3+1; AC 3 [16]; Atk 1 axe (1d8+1) or longbow (1d8); Move 12; Save 14; CL/XP 4/120; Special: Regenerate 2 hp/round (normal damage from fire).

Troll, Mimic

Mimic trolls are true horrors in all senses; besides their race's natural strength and toughness, they have the dreadful ability to assimilate the magical powers and effects they are affected with. Thus, a mimic troll affected by fire does not burn, but instead gains a fire attack form; a mimic troll cut in two by a blade not only rejoins its body but also gains a slashing attack, and so on. A mimic troll appears as a normal troll except for the many magical effects and special attacks assimilated into its body, which always manifest as noticeable physical mutations such as icicles on its skin, a fire aura, lightning eyes, +5 *vorpal* claws and the like.

Damage Source	Assimilated Power
Weapon	Claw takes the shape of the weapon and deals 1d8+1 points of damage.
Energy/Acid	Strike deals 1d6 points of same energy or acid damage.
Energy Drain	Troll's touch drains levels.
Poison	Touch deals same form of poison damage.

MIMIC TROLL: HD 9; AC 0 [19]; Atk 2 claws (1d8); Move 12; Save 7; CL/XP 11/1700; Special: Assimilate magic, regenerate 3 hp/rd (normal damage from fire).